Bolan was a split second too late

He reached out to grab the young woman's arm just as her hand closed around the doorknob. Star had already pushed open the door and started to speak when the first round exploded from inside the hostel office.

From where he stood next to the partially opened door, the Executioner couldn't see the gunman or any of the other men in the office. But he saw the result of the shot as it struck Star in the side of the neck and threw a fistful of flesh and blood back against the wall of the hallway.

The bullet ended Star's words in midsentence. As to her life, Bolan had no time to find out. He was too busy kicking the door fully open and drawing the Desert Eagle from under his vest.

MACK BOLAN ®
The Executioner

The Executioner®
Don Pendleton's

SPLINTER CELL

A GOLD EAGLE BOOK FROM
W♦RLDWIDE®

TORONTO • NEW YORK • LONDON
AMSTERDAM • PARIS • SYDNEY • HAMBURG
STOCKHOLM • ATHENS • TOKYO • MILAN
MADRID • WARSAW • BUDAPEST • AUCKLAND

First edition March 2007
ISBN-13: 978-0-373-64340-0
ISBN-10:   0-373-64340-3

Special thanks and acknowledgment to
Jerry VanCook for his contribution to this work.

SPLINTER CELL

Printed in U.S.A.

It is even better to act quickly and err than to hesitate until the time of action is past.
—Carl von Clausewitz, 1780–1831
On War

There is a time to contemplate and a time to take action. I am a man of action.
—Mack Bolan

THE
MACK BOLAN

LEGEND

Nothing less than a war could have fashioned the destiny of the man called Mack Bolan. Bolan earned the Executioner title in the jungle hell of Vietnam.

But this soldier also wore another name—Sergeant Mercy. He was so tagged because of the compassion he showed to wounded comrades-in-arms and Vietnamese civilians.

Mack Bolan's second tour of duty ended prematurely when he was given emergency leave to return home and bury his family, victims of the Mob. Then he declared a one-man war against the Mafia.

He confronted the Families head-on from coast to coast, and soon a hope of victory began to appear. But Bolan had broken society's every rule. That same society started gunning for this elusive warrior—to no avail.

So Bolan was offered amnesty to work within the system against terrorism. This time, as an employee of Uncle Sam, Bolan became Colonel John Phoenix. With a command center at Stony Man Farm in Virginia, he and his new allies—Able Team and Phoenix Force—waged relentless war on a new adversary: the KGB.

But when his one true love, April Rose, died at the hands of the Soviet terror machine, Bolan severed all ties with Establishment authority.

Now, after a lengthy lone-wolf struggle and much soul-searching, the Executioner has agreed to enter an "arm's-length" alliance with his government once more, reserving the right to pursue personal missions in his Everlasting War.

Prologue

The salt sea air mixed with the odor of fish grew stronger in Phil Paxton's nostrils as he made his final walk toward the Ijsselmeer. Amsterdam was different from what he'd expected it to be. No, he thought as he stopped along the concrete railing to gaze down one of the city's many canals, it wasn't Amsterdam that was different.

It was his *behavior* within the city that had surprised him.

Phil looked at his watch. He'd be back in New York by this time the following night. He was ready to get back. Not just ready but anxious. Phil Paxton was ready to go home. He was ready to marry Janie.

Taking in a final breath of sea air, Phil turned and retraced his steps toward the hotel. But when a passing taxi slowed he suddenly found himself waving it down. He still had several hours to kill before he headed to the airport.

"Rijksmuseum," he said as he got into the backseat.

The driver nodded, pulled away from the curb and reached forward and turned on the radio.

Phil closed his eyes and he pictured Janie as she had looked when she'd dropped him off at the airport two weeks earlier. Tears had trickled down her face, smearing her mascara and reddening her eyes. She had kissed him on the cheek rather than the mouth, then said softly, "Come back to me…if that's what you want to do." Then, without another word, she'd turned and walked away.

Pain seared through his heart as Phil opened his eyes again. They were passing a large park with grills set in concrete and bicycle paths. He could imagine families crowding around picnic tables, laughing, having fun, children racing about playing tag and other youthful games. He had told Janie that he had promised himself as a child that he would visit Amsterdam someday—*before* he got married. He had told her that he had always dreamed of visiting the Rembrandt House museum, the house where Anne Frank's family had hidden during the Nazi occupation, the step-gabled houses, historic churches and ancient towers.

The history of the city fascinated him. But that had not been his only reason for wanting to go to Amsterdam. And even though he hadn't told her, Janie knew it as well as he did.

The cabbie stopped at a red light, then turned right. Phil Paxton frowned. He would have sworn the Rijksmuseum was to the left. But what did he know? Maybe the cabdriver knew a shortcut. More likely, he knew a "long cut" that would increase the fare.

As the cab picked up speed, Phil closed his eyes again. Although Dutch painters and architecture had always been hobbies that bordered on passions with him, both he and Janie had known it was a very different kind of passion that had brought him to Amsterdam. Phil Paxton wanted to know for certain if he had finally settled down enough to get married. He didn't want to marry Janie only to find himself cheating on her two weeks later. He needed to find out if he could resist temptation. And few places in the world presented temptation in the form of beautiful and available women like Amsterdam.

Phil opened his eyes and was surprised to find that they

were in a section of the city he had not seen during his two weeks of furious touring. "Where are we?" he asked the driver.

The man glanced up into the rearview mirror. "Another fare to pick up," he said. "No worry. I charge you one-half only."

Phil shrugged. He had never liked arguing with people, especially with the additional complication of the language barrier. So he just closed his eyes again.

This time the smile that came to his face was genuine. He remembered the first night he had arrived in Amsterdam. Although he had caught a good six hours of sleep on the plane, and it had only been eight o'clock in the evening, he had convinced himself he was too tired to go looking for the fleshpots of the city. The next day he had spent several hours at the same museum toward which he was headed again now, eaten dinner at a small outdoor café, then returned to his hotel when the wine he'd drunk told him he was too woozy to get his money's worth from any of the prostitutes who had smiled at him on the sidewalks.

The third day he had gone to the Kalverstraut—the busiest shopping area in Holland. He had surprised himself when he'd returned to the hotel later that evening, unwrapped his purchases and suddenly realized they had all been presents for Janie.

So that night he had forced himself out of the hotel even though he hadn't wanted to go. He had made himself walk along the streets, eyeing the prostitutes who sat on display in the windows. Many were scantily clad. A few were completely nude. Without trying, he had found himself comparing each woman to Janie, and each time they came up short. Finally, he had come across a beautiful woman wearing a transparent negligee. Her long red hair fell past her shoulders and glimmered in the streetlights, and her skin was the color of milk. He had gone inside, paid the brothel owner for the entire night with her, then allowed the man to escort him to her room.

It was only after the man had shut the door on his way out, and the prostitute had let the negligee fall from her shoulders to the floor, that he had realized what had attracted him to her.

And why he could not go through with the act for which he had already paid.

The woman looked enough like Janie to be her sister.

Phil Paxton had left the room and taken a cab back to his hotel. The next day he had gone to one of Amsterdam's more famous diamond-cutters and had a stone cut and mounted in gold, doing his best to guess at exactly what Janie would like. And for the next week and a half, art, architecture and history *really had* become the reason for his trip.

His eyes still closed, Phil reached into the side pocket of his sport coat and felt the small felt-covered gift box that contained both Janie's engagement and wedding rings. In less than a day now, the engagement ring would be on her finger, and the thought made Phil's smile widen.

His thoughts were suddenly interrupted when the driver slammed on the brakes. Phil opened his eyes to see that they were no longer on the streets but had entered a dark alleyway that stank of garbage.

Then, as if on cue, the driver turned and aimed a pistol over the seat at his passenger. "Don't move," he said in a completely different accent than he had used earlier. "Or I'll kill you here and now."

A second later, white lights from outside the vehicle flooded the interior. Phil's door flew open and rough hands jerked him out. In a flash of vision, Phil Paxton saw rifle barrels and angry, dark-skinned faces. Then a hood was dropped over his head and tied in place around his neck with rope. Next he felt a hypodermic needle prick the skin on his upper arm.

A moment later, euphoria overcame Phil Paxton. For a

moment, he knew that whatever was happening had to be just fine. Everything would work out.

The euphoria, however, was short-lived. A few seconds later, he lost consciousness.

1

Only a highly trained soldier, cop or intelligence officer would have been likely to notice the differences. Tiny differences, like the fact that his bearing was slightly more erect, that he exuded more confidence than the average man. Or that the set of his jaw was a little firmer. But it was his eyes, he knew, that would have *really* given him away had he not taken great pains to keep anyone from staring into them. In those eyes other warriors could see that he'd seen hell, and lived to tell about it.

On the surface, however, Mack Bolan looked little different than any of the other men flying first class from New York. He wore a well-tailored gray pin-striped suit much like bankers, gem dealers and other businessmen wore when visiting Amsterdam. His passport claimed his name was Matt Cooper instead of Mack Bolan, or the more mysterious, and descriptive, appellation by which he was also known—the Executioner.

Bolan shifted slightly in his seat. He had felt tension in the air aboard the 747 ever since boarding. He had sensed that something was wrong ever since the plane had left the runway. Who knows *how* he knew—he just did.

The soldier leaned back against his seat and glanced to the man at his side, next to the window. The danger that filled the air was not coming from John "Brick" Paxton. Paxton had boarded the flight with the Executioner as his confederate rather than an adversary. Granted, accompanying Bolan had not been the former Army Ranger's idea; Paxton had made plans to rescue his younger brother, Phil, on his own. Just prior to boarding an earlier flight to the Netherlands, he'd been detained by representatives of Stony Man Farm, America's top-secret counterterrorist organization. The Farm's operatives had whisked Paxton away to a secluded safehouse while a secret meeting took place at the White House.

Bolan had been present at that meeting.

"There's no way to stop Brick Paxton from going after his brother short of throwing him in jail," the President told Hal Brognola, Stony Man Farm's director, as well as a high-ranking official at the Justice Department. "And I'm going to look like hell in the press if I jail a guy who's won two Silver Stars and is currently up for the Medal of Honor for his actions in Afghanistan and Iraq."

The Executioner watched as the Man nodded his way before concluding with, "So the best thing we can do is let him go after his brother. But I want Bolan with him."

Brognola nodded his agreement. "And I'd suggest sending them *immediately*, Mr. President," he said. "All of our intelligence at the moment indicates that the terrorists picked Phil Paxton at random, just because he was American. But sooner or later, they're going to find out just what a prize they've stumbled on to."

None of the three men had thought it necessary to further identify that "prize." They were all fully aware that Brick Paxton's younger brother was one of America's top nuclear engineers.

And a man who could build nukes for America could be forced to build them for America's enemies, as well.

The Executioner glanced out of the corner of his eye, studying Brick Paxton's face while he continued to review the past few hours in his mind. The Army Ranger's eyes were closed, but it was impossible to tell if he was asleep or not. He'd been against going with Bolan from the moment the idea had been presented to him, and had only agreed when it had finally become clear that the President *would* find a jail cell for him somewhere if he didn't.

Bolan turned back to the seat in front of him. The chain of command still wasn't fully clear in Paxton's mind. That might become a problem sooner or later. But the problem on the Executioner's mind at the moment came from somewhere else on the 747.

Dinner had been served aboard the plane a half hour earlier, and the remnants were still on the first-class passengers' trays. Lifting his plastic beverage glass, Bolan drained the contents, then he took the plastic fork and spoon from the table in front of him with his other hand and dropped them into the inside pocket of his jacket.

The ice at the bottom of his drink rattled as Bolan set the glass back down in the circular depression on the tray.

The flight attendant came quickly to his side. "Another Seven-Up, sir?" she asked with a suggestive smile. Her name tag read Margie.

Bolan's return smile was noncommittal. "No, thanks," he said. "I'm fine."

"And your friend?" Margie added.

Brick Paxton's eyes opened at the cue. "Sure. One more can't hurt."

Bolan sat quietly as Margie turned and disappeared into the galley between first class and the pilot's cabin. He had studied Brick Paxton's U.S. Army personnel file the day before and, among other things, learned that Paxton had a penchant for the bourbon. But nothing in the file suggested that he couldn't control his drinking, or ever drank to excess.

The flight attendant returned with another miniature bottle and a fresh glass of ice water. Placing them in front of Paxton, she removed the dinner trays in front of both men and disappeared into the galley once more.

Approximately fifteen minutes later, the man sitting directly across the aisle from Bolan unbuckled his seat belt and stood up. He had the dark skin and sharp features of a Middle Easterner. He reached up and opened the overhead storage compartment, then pulled down a black attaché case before closing the compartment.

Bolan had pinpointed the source of the tension that filled the air of the 747's first-class cabin. He watched the man out of the corner of his eye. It was not his race—the Executioner had worked with many men of Arabic origin in the past and knew that, as held true with any people, the good Arabs far outnumbered the bad. Nor was it the dark-skinned man's manner of dress that now caught Bolan's attention. It was not even the look in the man's eyes as he glanced quickly at Bolan before sitting down again, the attaché case on his lap.

Still, Bolan suddenly *knew.*

Bolan glanced over his shoulder. The curtain between first class and coach was drawn, but through the opening he could see that three other men—all looking to be of Middle Eastern origin like the man across from him—stood in the aisle. They had also opened the overhead storage compartments, and the Executioner watched as each pulled down a black attaché case identical to the one now in the lap of the man across from him.

Bolan felt his abdominal muscles tighten in anticipation. Four men. Four identical black attaché cases.

It was far too much to be coincidence.

The Executioner glanced to Paxton. The former Ranger

had just unscrewed the lid from his plastic shot bottle. But he had noted the man across from them, too, and while he couldn't see into the rear of the plane from his window seat, he'd caught the expression on Bolan's face.

"How many more?" Paxton whispered as he screwed the cap back onto his bottle of Wild Turkey and dropped it into the front pocket of his navy blue blazer.

"Three," the Executioner murmured. "All in coach. Same cases."

Brick Paxton nodded. He flipped his tray back up and out of the way into the seat in front of him, then began untying his right shoe.

The Executioner didn't have to ask what he was doing.

Bolan reached inside his jacket and felt his fingertips touch the tops of the plastic fork and spoon he had placed there earlier. He would have preferred to have his usual weapons—the Beretta 93-R and .44 Magnum Desert Eagle—but that had not been possible. Knowing that the enemy he would face once he reached Amsterdam closely watched incoming private flights, he and Paxton had chosen to fly commercial and were, therefore, unarmed.

At least conventionally unarmed. A man like the Executioner was *never completely without weapons*.

Leaving the plastic fork where it was, Bolan withdrew the spoon. Glancing casually across the aisle to make sure the man with the attaché case wasn't watching, he saw that sweat had broken out on the man's forehead. Dropping his hands beneath the table still in front of him, the Executioner twisted the head of the spoon until it broke off at a sharp angle. Discarding the rounded dipper end, he replaced the now sharp piece of plastic in his jacket.

By now Paxton had removed his right sock. Retrieving the

Wild Turkey bottle from his blazer pocket, he dropped it into the sock and tied a knot just above the small container.

Bolan folded his tray back up and pulled one of the in-flight magazines from the holder in front of him. Starting at the binding, he began rolling the periodical into the tightest tube he could fashion. Every few seconds, he used his peripheral vision to check on the man across the aisle. But the man with the attaché case was paying him no attention. He was far too engrossed in his own thoughts, and what he was about to do.

When the Executioner had finished rolling the magazine up, it was almost as hard as a length of wood. Pulling a pair of rubber bands from his pocket, he twisted them around the ends of the homemade bludgeon to keep the pages in place, then hid the club in the other inside pocket of his jacket, across from the fork and broken spoon.

Paxton's makeshift sap was finished, too, and the Army Ranger glanced across the aisle before slapping the sock-covered bottle into the palm of his opposite hand. Satisfied, he tied his shoe back onto his bare foot.

"We don't know what's in the attaché cases yet," Bolan whispered. "Maybe guns. Maybe a bomb. Maybe both." He let out a breath. "Our only chance is to get the jump on them."

"And if they turn out to be just four Arabic businessmen who happen to have the same kind of briefcases?" Paxton asked.

"We'll apologize," Bolan said. "And offer to pay the hospital bill for them."

Paxton chuckled, low and deep. "That's not going to be the case, though, is it," he said in a tone of voice that made his words a statement rather than a question.

"No," the Executioner said. He unbuckled his seat belt. "I'm heading to the coach cabin. You concentrate on the man here in first class."

Paxton's eyebrows lowered. "You're gonna take out *three*

of them?" he said. "No, I'll go with you. We'll get those three, then—"

"We don't have time to argue," Bolan ordered. "If we're both in the back, and this clown across from us has a bomb, he's only a few steps from the pilot. And he'll get plenty of warning if there's a scuffle behind him."

Paxton saw the logic in the Executioner's plan. He nodded.

Bolan stood up. The man with the attaché case had glanced at his watch twice before Bolan could even turn down the aisle away from the cabin.

Whatever the four men were planning was about to go down. *Soon.*

The flight attendant seemed to appear from nowhere as Bolan stepped through the door from first class to coach. "Oh, sir," Margie said, bumping into him. "I'm sorry."

"No problem," said the Executioner, and started to step around her.

"Sir, where are you going?"

"Restroom," Bolan said, again trying to step to the side in the narrow aisle.

"But there's a much better one in first class," Margie said.

"It's taken," Bolan said. Beyond the flight attendant, he saw sweat and tension on the faces of the other three men who had pulled the attaché cases down from the overhead compartments. As the nervous man in first class had done, they all glanced at their wristwatches.

Then three hands moved to the latches on the cases.

Bolan shoved Margie to the side and sprinted down the aisle. Whatever was about to happen was no longer about to happen *soon.*

It was happening *now.*

THE THREE Arabs all looked up at the big man running toward them, and Bolan was reminded that the almost supernatural sense of danger was never limited to the good guys. Criminals, terrorists and other miscreants developed it just like good soldiers, cops and other warriors.

A glint of fire suddenly appeared in the eyes of the three men. They stood up as they opened their cases.

Bolan continued to run down the aisle past the curious faces of the other passengers. He still didn't know what was in the black attaché cases. But it was a good bet that it would be either guns, bombs or both. Neither did he know how the terrorists had gotten the cases past security and on board the plane.

But that hardly mattered now. The reality of the situation was that they *had* gotten the cases onto the plane, and he would have to deal with that reality as it stood. If guns were their only weapons, he stood a good chance of saving the hundreds of people on board the 747. But if there were four bombs on the plane, not even the Executioner would be able to get to them all before at least one was detonated.

Bolan didn't break stride as he drew the broken plastic spoon from his pocket and drove the sharp point into the dark-skinned throat above the SIG-Sauer pistol his adversary had pulled from the attaché case. A chortling sound issued forth with the blood that shot out of the man's jugular vein, staining his white shirt and beige suit. The Executioner reached out, grabbing for the SIG-Sauer.

He was a split second too late.

Waving his arms wildly in the throes of death, the would-be gunman released the SIG. It flew out over the passengers and fell somewhere behind Bolan.

The black attaché case dropped to the deck of the plane, open. Two shirts and a pair of slacks flew out from between the sides. But no bomb.

The terrorist in the beige suit fell to the floor on top of the mess.

Bolan leaped over the still-convulsing body and continued down the aisle, jerking the tightly wrapped magazine from inside his jacket as he ran. By now, the second man—wearing a light blue suit and darker blue necktie—had pulled a Glock from his attaché case. His hand shook nervously as he tried to steady his aim on the Executioner.

Bolan ducked low, praying that like most nervous men, the would-be hijacker would shoot high. Not just high enough to miss him, but high enough to miss all of the seated passengers as well.

His prayer was answered.

The Glock exploded with an almost deafening roar in the tight confines of the cabin. More screams threatened to burst the Executioner's eardrums. But Bolan could tell by the angle of the barrel that the shot had gone to the ceiling and exited the plane. The hole it made was far too small to affect the cabin pressure. But too many of the passengers had seen movies where such tiny openings sucked everyone out into the sky, and more panicky screams added to the chaos around Bolan.

Bolan didn't give the man with the Glock a second chance. With a sudden leap, he reached the terrorist and swung the rolled magazine like a short billy club. The hardened pages caught the man in the Adam's apple and crushed his larynx. Bolan followed through with a left hook, connecting with the man's temple with the force of a jackhammer.

The Glock fell to the seat behind the terrorist. The man's lifeless body began to fall backward on top of it.

Bolan reached out, grabbing the second terrorist by the shoulders and throwing him to the other side of the aisle, out of the way. But when he looked down to the seat for the Glock, it was gone.

But the Executioner had no time to waste. Rather than

go searching for the Glock, the Executioner continued down the aisle until the final terrorist in coach class shouted in heavily accented English, "Halt! Stop now, or I will blow up the plane!"

Still a good twenty feet from the man, Bolan could see the arrogant smile on his face. He wore a black suit with light pinstripes. He had opened his attaché case and turned it to face the Executioner.

Bolan stared into the open case. This man had no pistol for him to worry about.

What he did have, however, was a bomb.

The Executioner stood motionless as the terrorist had ordered. "What is it you want?"

"First," the man with the bomb said sarcastically, "is for all of these swine to...*shut up!*" He shouted the last two words at the top of his lungs. And they had the desired effect. The last of the screaming, moaning and crying turned to an eerie silence as the passengers quieted, frozen in fear.

"All right," Bolan said, standing upright in the center of the aisle. "You got your first wish. Now what?" He stared into the open attaché case, trying to make out the details of the bomb under the shadows created by the lid. He couldn't be sure but it looked as if the case contained a substantial amount of plastic explosive—probably Semtex. The shiny, polished steel of what had to be a detonator flashed at him. The item most easy to see and recognize was a common digital kitchen timer.

There didn't look to be anything high-tech about the explosive device. It was simple. Very simple.

But still *lethal*.

Satisfied that Bolan had seen what was in the case, the terrorist in the black suit now closed it partway but kept his left hand inside.

The Executioner gauged the distance between him and the

terrorist. If he had judged the design of the bomb correctly during the second or so he'd been allowed to view it, it should be easy enough to defuse. *If* he could get to it before the man in the black suit set it off.

But that wasn't likely. The same simplicity that made it easy to neutralize also made it easy and fast to detonate. The timer was electronic, and made no ticking sound. So it was impossible to determine if it had been set or not. But that made little difference, either. All it would take to override the timing device would be to touch two wires together, and Bolan could see by the way the terrorist's hand was positioned that he held one of those wires inside the half-closed case even now.

The man with the bomb had not replied to Bolan's question, so the Executioner repeated it. "What do you want now?" he said in a louder voice.

"I want you to sit down," said the dark-featured man.

"This has got to be a give-and-take negotiation," Bolan said, speaking for all of the passengers. "What do we get in return?" Bolan asked, playing for time.

He continued to stare the terrorist in the eye. If he was to have any chance at all of reaching the attaché case before the bomb went off, he needed the terrorist in the black suit to be distracted in as many ways as possible.

He was about to speak again—simply to buy more time—when he felt a light tapping on his left hip. Slowly glancing down to his side, the Executioner saw a little girl who could have been no more than eight years old. She wore a frilly pink-and-white dress, white anklets rolled down and black buckled shoes. Her sandy-blond hair was pulled back into a tight ponytail.

On the little girl's face, Bolan saw terror. In her left hand was a Barbie doll with hair that matched her own.

But in her right hand was the barrel of the Glock.

Whoever had come into possession of the pistol after it had been thrown over the seats had determined that Bolan was on their side. The gun had been passed clandestinely to the passenger nearest Bolan, and that had been the little blond girl.

Bolan felt the hard plastic Glock in his fist as the little girl released the barrel.

"You saw what happened to the other men back here in coach," the Executioner said to the terrorist. "But don't you wonder about the man you had in first class?"

Bolan wondered, too. But it appeared that Paxton had taken care of the terrorist who had first given himself away to the Executioner. At least there had been no shots fired from the front of the craft. And no explosions.

As soon as the words had left the Executioner's mouth, the man with the bomb glanced past him toward first class.

Bolan knew it was the best distraction he could pull off.

He brought the Glock out from behind the seat and snapped it up, pointing the barrel as if it were his finger and depressing the trigger at the same time. He saw the red hole appear in the forehead of the terrorist. At almost the same time the back of the man's head blew out.

The screams, cries and moans returned as Bolan sprinted forward. The attaché case had fallen to the middle of the aisle, and now he dropped to one knee to look inside. His heart fell to his stomach when he saw that what had looked like a simple device from a distance was actually somewhat more complex.

At least a dozen wires—all in different colors—from the Semtex through the detonator to the timer. Most would be dummies that would have no effect at all if cut. But one would be an instant detonator that would override the timer and set off the plastic explosive immediately.

None of which would have been a problem if the timer wasn't set. Bolan could simply fold the attaché case back up, take it to his seat and turn it over to Dutch authorities when they landed in Amsterdam.

But all hope of such a simple end to the problem flew from the Executioner's thoughts as he looked at the timer. It *had* been set.

And the bomb was going to explode in 43 seconds.

THE EXECUTIONER REACHED down and lifted the kitchen timer in his hand, taking a long shot and simply pushing the start-stop button. As he'd suspected, it changed nothing. It had obviously been disconnected somewhere inside because the seconds continued ticking away.

By now, many of the passengers had recovered from shock. Questions assaulted him from all sides. Several of the passengers had unbuckled their seat belts and were starting to rise, curious to see what was inside the attaché case and what the Executioner was doing.

"Sit down! Everybody!" Bolan called out in a loud, authoritative voice that caused the men and women to drop immediately back down into their seats. As he turned back toward the front of the plane, he saw both Paxton and Margie running down the aisle to meet him. Paxton had another SIG-Sauer jammed into his belt, which could only mean that he'd successfully neutralized the first terrorist they'd spotted in first class.

Margie looked puzzled. But Paxton took it all in immediately. "How long have we got?" he asked.

The Executioner glanced back down to the timer. "Thirty-eight seconds," he said. Turning his eyes quickly to Margie, he said, "Tell the captain to unlock the master lock to the main door in first class." Margie started to turn.

"And tell him to slow speed to the bare minimum," the Executioner added.

The woman nodded as she ran back in the direction from which she'd come.

"You're going to try to throw that thing out the door?" Paxton asked incredulously.

"That's the plan."

"You open that door at this speed and altitude and you'll get sucked out of the plane," Paxton warned.

"That's why I told her to have the pilot slow down," Bolan said.

Paxton and Bolan sprinted back through the coach cabin into first class.

Bolan addressed the six men who were still seated there, their eyes wide in fear. "Quick! I need you to take off your belts and give them to me."

Immediately, the men unbuckled themselves and began sliding their belts out of their pants. While they were so engaged, the Executioner turned back to Margie. "Get on the phone and tell the captain to drop the oxygen masks. It'll give the passengers something to do," he explained.

When the Executioner had gathered all six of the belts, he tossed three of them to Paxton. The Ranger had figured out what he had planned and he buckled one strip of leather through his own belt, then began linking the others together. Bolan did the same with the three belts in his hands, hoping the buckles and any other weak spots in the leather would hold.

The Executioner linked his last belt to that of Paxton's, then turned to the cabin door. He had just enough length in the makeshift retention straps to reach the handle. Swiftly twisting it, he heard the whir of a million bees' wings as he slid the door open. At the same time, he felt himself suddenly pulled forward. His own belt, attached to the leather chain, threatened to cut him in two the waist. He swallowed hard, trying to equalize the pressure in his ears as the atmosphere suddenly changed. Glancing downward, he saw that he had eight seconds left on the timer. He swallowed hard again. Even if the bomb didn't explode, it felt as if his eardrums would.

Taking a final look down at the timer, the Executioner saw only the number 4. Before it could turn to 3, he leaned forward, assisted by the vacuum, and pushed the attaché case through the opening.

A second later, a barely audible popping sound issued forth through the galelike wind outside the doorway. The sound was so small—so seemingly insignificant in the distance—that it was almost an anticlimax to the near destruction and deaths it had almost caused. Bolan closed the door.

The threat was over. For now, at least.

But as the Executioner walked back and dropped into his seat, he knew that while his actions had saved the lives of the several hundred people on the plane, he had been unsuccessful in at least one way.

He and Paxton had flown commercial to keep a low profile upon entering the Netherlands. There was no chance of that now. By the time they touched down in Amsterdam the pilot would have radioed all that had happened aboard the 747 to the tower. There would be long interviews with police, which took time away from the mission. But worse than that, the airport would be a carnival of newsmen and -women shouting questions and popping flash in their faces.

Bolan and Brick Paxton would not go unnoticed, they'd be celebrities. Their pictures would be on the front page of every newspaper in Europe and quite possibly the rest of the world.

The Executioner leaned back against his seat, shut his eyes

and frowned. Then, slowly, the corners of his mouth began to turn upward as a plan took shape in his mind.

A LIGHT SNOW HAD BEGUN falling over the city of Marken by the time Abdul Hassan slid his heavy overcoat over his navy blue blazer, placed the woven tweed fedora on his head and wrapped his muffler around his neck. He descended the back stairs of his hotel to avoid having to speak to the desk clerk but, as luck would have it, the hotel manager was sweeping the stairwell near the rear door when he reached the ground floor.

The manager looked up in surprise when he heard Hassan's footsteps coming down the last flight of stairs. But he smiled. "It is not *that* cold outside," he said in Dutch as he dumped the contents of his dustpan into the large rubber trash can he had rolled into the stairwell along with the broom. "You will soon be sweating."

Hassan forced a laugh. He didn't like surprises like this, didn't like being noticed at all when he was in Marken. Which was why, while he lived only a few short miles away in Amsterdam, he always came to town the night before he was to meet his contact. And why he never stayed at the same hotel. But such coincidences were sometimes unavoidable, and he had his cover story ready, as always.

"You seem to forget," Hassan replied in Dutch, "that I come from a country where 120-degree temperatures are not unusual. To me, it is *freezing* out there."

The two exchanged another short, polite round of laughter. As Hassan reached for the door, the manager's eyebrows lowered in either concern or curiosity—Hassan wasn't sure which. But he expressed concern.

"You should use the front door," the man said. "Marken is

not a violent town like Amsterdam. Still, there is crime, and the alleys are not safe."

Hassan shrugged. "I suppose you are right," he said. "But I am only out for a short walk. And it is only a few steps down the alley from the door to the street. I will be all right."

Now it was the manager's turn to shrug. "Suit yourself," he said. "But I will watch you from the door until you reach the sidewalk."

"Thank you," Hassan said and opened the door.

The manager had been correct—it was not cold enough outside for the way Abdul Hassan had dressed. He guessed the temperature to be only slightly below freezing, and the wind was light. Still, it chilled his face and hands as he stepped outside. His footsteps echoed hollowly along the bricks of the narrow alleyway, and he could see the light from the open door to the hotel reflecting off the walls to both his sides. It illuminated his path, and for that he was grateful.

He glanced behind him and saw that, as promised, the hotel manager was still watching him.

He walked casually along the pavement. He would take a roundabout route through the downtown area of Marken, doing his best to appear to be nothing more than his cover story claimed he was—an exporter of Holland's wooden shoes to the Middle East. He was in town on business and bored in his hotel room.

The real reason for his walk, however, was to look for a tail. He had begun his relationship with the Central Intelligence Agency nearly three years before, which was a long time for such a relationship. He was only human, and he knew he had made many mistakes in the past that could have given him away to the more fundamentalist Muslims who had infiltrated Amsterdam and the rest of the Netherlands. What was even more frightening was the fact that he knew he had to have made countless other mistakes of which he was not even aware.

Perhaps it was time to get out. On the other hand, he wasn't sure he could do that. He felt a tremendous responsibility to stop the terrorism his misguided fellow Arabs perpetrated. It gave everyone with the sharp features and dark skin of the Middle East a bad name, and made men and women suspicious of everyone who fit the profile.

Hassan didn't even glance into the shoe-shop window as he passed. If someone was following him, he didn't want the man remembering him as having any interest in the shoe shop at all. Tomorrow, he would leave through the same door to the alley by which he'd exited the hotel tonight, then follow a labyrinth of other alleys to another back door into the shoe shop.

There, he knew, he was to meet two *new* men.

The snow began to lighten as Abdul Hassan walked on, stopping occasionally to window-shop at businesses that had nothing to do with his work, and glancing casually behind him. He did the same at street corners as he waited for traffic lights to change, and turned randomly right and left whenever the mood struck him, or when he thought he'd seen a familiar figure behind him more than once. Each time, the men or women who had caught his attention eventually disappeared. Which meant that he was left wondering if he had simply imagined them following him, or if they might have turned the surveillance over to another agent.

Yes, Abdul Hassan nodded to himself as he finally turned back toward his hotel. Paranoia was definitely beginning to get the better of him.

But by the time he was within two blocks of his hotel, his mistrust had all but evaporated. He had seen no one on the way back that he had seen before, and he felt a sudden relaxation come over him. Either no one was interested in him, or they were so good at what they did that he would never spot them. If the latter was the case, there was nothing he could do about it. They would eventually kill him, and that would be that. Strangely, this realization brought on a certain calmness. He had done everything he could do.

Hassan slowed his pace, actually enjoying the walk now that he had given up his own counter-surveillance and warmed up. He stuffed his hands deeper into his coat pockets and felt the hilt of the *pesh kabz* dagger. The T-shaped blade was always reassuring to him. Even though it was of Persian and Northern India origin and he was not, he had chosen it because its original role had been to penetrate chain mail.

He assumed it would work just as well in penetrating the thick clothing worn against the Netherlands cold. He always carried the dagger unsheathed, letting the heavy wool of his coat and the other layers of clothing beneath the garment protect him from both the point and edges.

Hassan wrapped his fingers around the grip of the dagger as he walked on. There were two reasons he had left Syria for the Netherlands. The first was to escape the influence of the fundamentalist Muslims who insisted on restricting behavior to that more befitting the twelfth century than the twenty-first. The second reason was the heat. What he sometimes questioned, however, was why he had allowed himself to be recruited by Jim Campbell, who had been the CIA chief of station in Amsterdam when he'd first arrived. What was even more puzzling was why he'd stayed on after Campbell had been transferred and he'd been turned over to the ambitious man's lackluster replacement, Felix Young.

Hassan thought of the man who had taken Campbell's place. He rarely left his office, wherever that was—Hassan had to assume it was at the American Embassy after the fashion of all intelligence services the world over. The bottom line was that Hassan had done more work, accomplished far more, during the six months he'd worked for Campbell than in the two and a half years since his recruiter had been replaced.

The light turned and Abdul Hassan walked on. He could see the sign above his hotel ahead. Soon he would be inside and warm. He would get a good night's rest, then meet with two new men from some other agency to which the CIA was turning him over. He hoped they would be more ambitious than Young, and that he would actually do some good in changing the way the world looked at Islam and Arabs at this point in history. As his heels clicked against the concrete, he thought of his own feelings of religion. He was hardly a man without sin, and he had always been especially susceptible to one sin in particular. His was a *major* sin for which he not only felt guilty but for which he might fall victim to death just as fast as he would if the terrorist faction in the Netherlands ever found out he was an informant for the Americans.

This thought not only sent guilt coursing through Hassan's veins, but also it brought fear. And it was right in the middle of this fear that an arm suddenly reached out from a darkened doorway fifty feet from his hotel and jerked him off the sidewalk into the darkness.

Hassan smelled the strong odor of curry on his assailant's breath. "Die, you bastard!" he heard a gruff voice say in Arabic.

A split second after that, something pushed hard against the side of his coat. Then it felt as if a pin or needle had pricked the bare skin beneath his garments.

Instinctively, Hassan drew the dagger from his coat pocket in a reverse grip. He could feel something still tangled in his overcoat as he reached up and wrapped his left arm around the back of his attacker's neck. The Persian dagger rose high over his head, then came down with all of the force he could muster from his arm and shoulder, penetrating the other man's clothing, skin, and burying itself deep within his heart.

Fear, anger and adrenaline now mixed in Abdul Hassan's soul as he withdrew the dagger. He brought it up into the air

once more, then thrust it down again as close to the same spot
as he could. The man who had tried to kill him went limp in
his arms, then slumped to the ground inside the doorway.

Hassan knelt, grabbed a sleeve of the man's coat and used it
to wipe the splattered blood from his face. His heart still beating
like a kettle drum inside his chest, Hassan stood back up. He
knew his coat would be soaked in blood so he would use the same
side entrance to the hotel, secure in the fact that since the manager
had already swept there it would be vacant now. He peered out
from the doorway, looking quickly up and down the sidewalk.

There was no one else in sight.

Pulling a small penlight from the inside breast pocket of
his overcoat, Hassan shone the tiny beam onto the dead
features of the man he had just killed. The man's eyes were
open, staring lifelessly back at him.

But Hassan didn't recognize the face. So he had no idea
whether the attempted murder had come from his association
with the CIA or from his private sin.

Using the penlight now to check himself, in addition to the
blood Hassan saw that the hilt of a broad-bladed dagger still
extended from his coat just beyond where he had felt the
pinprick. He pulled out the knife and saw only the tiniest
drop of blood on the tip. The wide, leaf-shaped blade had been
a poor choice for assassination through heavy clothing.

It was not the kind of weapon a professional killer would
choose on a cold night when men wore heavy layers of
clothing. Which led him to believe the would-be assassin was
an amateur, and that, in turn, answered his earlier question.

His relationship with the Americans was still secure. This
attack was directly related to his personal sin rather than his
work for them.

The man lying dead in the doorway had come to kill him
for reasons personal rather than political.

2

"They told me you speak Dutch and Arabic," Bolan said to Paxton as he grabbed the man's elbow and pointed him toward the passenger terminal's freight reception area in the distance. They had excited the plane through a hatch that led to the cargo hold, where they donned the overalls that baggage handlers wore.

"More Dutch than Arabic," the Army Ranger said. "I'm not exactly what you'd call fluent in either. But I can hear enough Dutch right now to know that everybody—cops, reporters and airport officials—are all looking for us. The passengers are keeping their word and covering for us, saying we're getting off last."

"That should give us some time, then," the Executioner said. "Come on."

They quickly reached the freight area, where they passed several other men dressed in similar coveralls. The men didn't give them a second look. Ducking into a stairwell to the side of the large room, Bolan led Paxton up the steps to the next landing and peered through a window in the door. What he saw looked more like a freight expedition area than what he wanted, so he said, "Let's try one more level."

The two men jogged up the next flight of steps, taking them two at a time.

This time, the Executioner looked through the window and saw what appeared to be a boarding room. Quickly stripping off their coveralls, he and Paxton dropped them in the stairwell and stepped out onto the carpet.

The excitement created by the attempted hijacking hadn't seemed to reach this level of the terminal yet, and Bolan led the way past a duty-free shop and several ticket desks to a sign that read *Passport Control* in a variety of languages. He waited as an elderly couple got their passports stamped, then stepped up to the desk and pulled his own small blue book from inside his coat.

The uniformed man behind the counter glanced at the picture in the American passport, then Bolan's face, and asked in English, "Business or pleasure, Mr. Cooper?"

"Primarily business," Bolan answered. Then he smiled. "But I've never been to Amsterdam without having a good time, either."

The uniformed official chuckled under his breath, stamped the passport and handed it back. "Have fun," he said.

Bolan waited to the side as Brick Paxton handed the same man the passport Stony Man Farm had come up with for him. He was traveling under the name John Henry McBride, who was a general building contractor. The Executioner had learned that Paxton had worked construction during the summers when he'd been in high school, and had more than a passing knowledge of the business. So that was to be both men's cover from now on. If anyone asked, they were in the Netherlands to check into both commercial and residential construction for the Brown Realty Holdings Company, out of Chicago, Illinois.

As soon as "McBride's" passport had been stamped they were waved quickly through customs. They didn't look like drug smugglers, but it wouldn't have mattered much if they had in a country where most drugs were legal. The nonchalance shown by the Dutch customs officers reminded the Executioner of an old saying among drug abusers: "Taking your own dope to Amsterdam is like taking your wife to Paris."

An elevator took them back down to the ground level, and they stepped out through the revolving doors of the terminal. Two minutes later Bolan had flagged down a cab. The cabbie took one look at the two men and immediately sized them up as Americans. "No luggage?" he asked in a thick Dutch accent.

Bolan shook his head. "We shipped it ahead of us."

The cabbie wore a plaid driving cap with a short bill as he got back inside behind the wheel. "Where to?" he asked.

"The American Embassy," the Executioner said.

The driver glanced up into the rearview mirror, the fact that he was impressed evident in his eyes. Without another word, he threw the cab into Drive and took off at breakneck speed, dodging in, out and around other vehicles with the daring for which certain cabdrivers are known the world over.

Forty-five minutes later they came to a screeching halt beneath an American flag mounted atop a pole sticking up out of a thick concrete wall. It waved in the breeze as if welcoming them as they got out.

Two U.S. Marine Corpsmen stood guard at the gate. Bolan and Paxton showed the men their passports. One of the Marines checked the list on the clipboard in the guard cubicle just inside the walls, then opened the gate and waved them in. The other Marine escorted them up a set of steps and into the building. He knocked loudly on a first-floor door at the rear of the embassy and waited for it to be opened.

When the door was answered, a short, overweight man chewing on one of the earpieces of a pair of reading glasses stood just inside the office.

"Mr. Cooper and Mr. McBride," the Marine said. Then,

with a stiff salute, he pivoted away from them and marched back down the hall.

"Come in. My name is Felix Young," the short man said with one of the least enthusiastic tones of voice Bolan had ever heard. He was dressed in brown slacks below a pale blue sweater vest, with white shirt sleeves rolled up past his elbows. The knot of his necktie had been pulled down almost to the end of the V in the vest, and his general appearance was one of slovenliness. The office was in a similar state, with stacks of paper cluttering his desk, several tables and the tops of a half-dozen filing cabinets. Ashtrays scattered throughout the room overflowed with cigarette butts, and the stale smell of smoke hung in the air like the fog of a London morning.

Bolan's eyes fell to a stack of luggage in the corner of the office. The suitcases and other bags were the only items in the office not covered in a thin coat of gray ash—which meant they couldn't have been in the room very long. They likely contained Bolan's and Paxton's clothing and other gear, including their weapons, all of which had been flown over from America in diplomatic pouches.

Felix Young dropped into his seat behind the desk. Bolan and Paxton both looked around, but the chairs in front of the desk were as cluttered with paperwork as the rest of the furniture so they remained standing.

"I don't know exactly who you are," Young said in a tone that had only slightly more character and inflection in it than had his self-introduction. "And I don't know exactly why you're here." He opened the top middle drawer of his desk, retrieved a crumpled package of unfiltered cigarettes. When he'd lit a cigarette, he went on. "And I'm not sure I *want* to know." He drew in a lungful of smoke and looked up at the ceiling with complete uninterest.

Bolan was quickly tiring of the listless bureaucrat. The man was CIA—that much he knew because Hal Brognola had told him. As to any further information about Felix Young, the Executioner could only guess that he was nearing retirement, had lost all enthusiasm for his work and would be happy as long as the two men standing in front of his desk didn't create any extra work for him.

Young more or less voiced those thoughts himself by saying, "Keep in mind that whatever you do here, we're going to get blamed for it." He looked down from the ceiling but met Bolan's eyes for only a second before turning his gaze to a wall. "CIA, CIA, CIA," he breathed out with another chestful of smoke. "The whole world blames everything that happens on the CIA."

Paxton was losing patience with the man, too. "I don't see how they could blame too much on *you*," he said.

Young merely pointed toward the luggage. "All of your stuff is in the corner there," he said. "So just take it."

Paxton moved toward the bags but Bolan stayed in place. "I believe you have something else for us," he said.

Young frowned. It was obvious his mind had already moved from Bolan and Paxton to something else. "Oh," he finally said. "Yeah." Opening the same drawer where he'd found the cigarettes, he pulled out a crumpled scrap of paper and spread it out on the desk. Pushing it down with both hands in an attempt to flatten it, he finally lifted the paper again and handed it across the desk to Bolan. "Here. Try not to burn the guy, okay?"

Bolan stuffed the rumpled page into his pocket. He couldn't see how burning the informant Young was turning over to him would have much effect on the listless CIA man one way or another. It could get the snitch killed, of course. But it didn't appear that the man behind the desk planned on using him any more than he had to. Or doing anything else that required any effort, either.

Without further words, Bolan joined Paxton and the two men lifted the various bags from the corner of the office and left. The Executioner felt both disgust and relief as they walked back down the hall. The disgust came from seeing a man like Young who had lost all enthusiasm for his work and now did nothing but punch the time clock while he waited for retirement. But the fact that the CIA officer didn't appear to have any plans of interfering with what he and Paxton were about to do was a relief.

THERE HAD BEEN no euphoria left in him by the time Phil Paxton awakened.

Only terror.

Phil looked around the semilit room as he came to his senses and wondered if he might not still be asleep. Was this a dream? He closed his eyes once more, hoping it was. But the reality of the situation, and the memory of what had happened, came flooding back to his mind and forced his eyelids open again.

The undisputed realization that the room he was in was a *cell* hit him between the eyes like a two-by-four. The walls were made of jagged stone, and overhead he saw rough-hewn wooden beams. It looked like something out of a horror movie, a place where Frankenstein's monster might live, or where Dracula might keep his coffin to sleep in during the daylight. Maybe where the Wolfman would chain himself up during full moons in the hope that the chains might prevent him from ripping people apart with his long teeth and fangs.

The thought of chains led Phil Paxton to look down at the steel handcuffs encircling his wrists. The chain between the two cuffs was attached to another chain that ran around his waist. That restraint, in turn, was secured by a large sturdy padlock.

Phil Paxton's back and legs felt as if they were in ice packs.

Looking down, he saw that he was seated on the smoother stone of the floor. A painful twist of his cold and stiff neck told him his back rested against the wall, and condensation glistening off the stones had soaked through his shirt. For some reason, that sudden knowledge—that his shirt was wet and likely to remain that way—caused him to shiver more than any other of the morbid details that were just now registering with him.

As Phil continued to shake with both cold and fear, his mind began to race. Where the hell was he? He had been kidnapped, he remembered, as the events that had taken place before he lost consciousness suddenly flooded back into his memory. The taxi. The alley. The lights from outside and suddenly being jerked out of the vehicle. The hood coming down over his head and then the needle in his arm, which brought on elation and then oblivion.

But who had kidnapped him? And what did they want?

In the back of his sluggish brain an alarming possibility began to take shape. Phil repressed the thought as long as he could, concentrating again on his surroundings. A thick wooden door that looked centuries old—and added to the Saturday-afternoon horror-film atmosphere—stood a few feet away, to his left. A small window had been cut in the upper part of the door. The opening was too small for a man to even get his head through, but for some reason the builders had still seen fit to equip it with tiny iron bars. The bars were red with rust and looked as if they had been in place for centuries. Through this small window came what little light illuminated the cell. And with that light came the minute amount of hope that was still in Phil Paxton's soul.

The chained man stared at the door. In the silence that surrounded him, he could hear his own breathing. But now and then, as if far in the distance, he caught the sounds of a few words being passed back and forth between different voices. How many voices, and how many men, he couldn't tell. But it sounded as if they were just outside his cell, whispering. Phil almost laughed out loud in his near hysteria. Why would they bother to whisper? Were they afraid he might overhear something they didn't want him to hear? Maybe some magic formula with which he could break free of his bonds and escape? The whispering didn't make sense—particularly since it was in a language he didn't understand.

But a language that suddenly, either by instinct or having heard it spoken somewhere before, he knew was Arabic.

Now the possibility he had so far suppressed bulled its way to the front of his brain with the force of a freight train. Again, he felt as if a large board or baseball bat had struck him between the eyes. The men who had snatched him out of the cab were Arabs, and the accent to which the cabdriver had changed when he'd threatened to shoot him had been Middle Eastern, too. He had been kidnapped by Islamic fundamentalist terrorists. Exactly which faction they represented, he didn't know.

Phil Paxton's shoulders shivered even harder now, as if he were doing the jitterbug or some other strange dance. The Netherlands, he knew, was awash with Middle Eastern terrorists these days. They had murdered Dutch officials, set off suicide bombs in government buildings and other sites, and kidnapped tourists to hold for ransom.

And Americans, as always, were their number-one choice for kidnapping.

Phil leaned forward in an attempt to stop shaking. He knew from news reports that even when the ransoms were paid, most of the victims—and *always* the Americans—were still murdered. Some had even been shown being beheaded by huge swords on the Internet.

Now the chill spread from Phil's back and shoulders through the rest of his body. He felt as if the blood in his veins and arteries had suddenly frozen to ice from the top of his head to the bottoms of his feet.

But even being American, he realized, was not his biggest liability. He was a *very special* kind of American—different from the men and women from the U.S. who had been the victims of terrorist kidnappings before him. They had been taken at random without regard for their professions. They had been simple people—businessmen, housewives, low- to mid-level government employees, men and women with no particular talents or expertise that could benefit the terrorists.

Phil Paxton didn't fall into that category, and he knew it. But did his captors? Did they know what he did for a living? Had he been snatched up indiscriminately, simply as a target of opportunity like the others, or had he been kidnapped on purpose for the expertise he could provide? And even if the men who had imprisoned him didn't now know who he was and what he did for a living, would they find out? And when they did, could they force him through torture to do their bidding?

A collage of horrifying images suddenly filled his brain. Phil saw pictures of Janie wearing her engagement ring, then himself being beheaded while millions of people watched on the Internet, then Janie wearing black and attending his funeral. He saw his brother, Brick—wearing camouflage clothing, his face blackened with nonreflective makeup—firing a rifle and mowing down the men who held him prisoner. Then he saw himself in a rude, makeshift laboratory, working on a crude device on a table while heavily bearded men wearing the long flowing headdresses known as *kaffiyehs* stood to his side, aiming guns at his head.

For a moment, Phil thought he would scream. Then he felt his brows furrow into a frown as he did his best to break through the freezing terror and bring himself back into the rational realm that was his room. If he was to survive the situation in which he now found himself, that survival could only come by getting a grip on himself. He would have to control—even ignore—the fear and these fear-induced images.

Phil forced himself to close his eyes and concentrate on his breathing. He rolled his eyeballs back in his head, then tightened his abdominal muscles. It was an ancient warrior trick he had learned from Brick. While it didn't drive *all* of the fear from his soul, it relaxed him enough to begin thinking logically again.

Phil Paxton couldn't reach the back pocket of the jeans he was wearing where he kept his leather passport case. But by rolling onto his hip, he was able to determine that it was gone. That was to be expected. The terrorists—from whatever Islamic fundamentalist group they were from—would naturally have taken it. And in addition to his passport, they would find the other items he had transferred from the billfold he usually carried when he was at home.

But had his U.S. government ID been in his passport case? He couldn't remember now if he had brought it along. Which meant he had no way of knowing whether the men who had kidnapped him knew he was one of America's top nuclear scientists. And that he was more than capable of building either nuclear bombs or putting together "dirty bombs" if they didn't have all of the components necessary to produce a real nuke.

The shivering returned to his shoulders, and Phil rolled his eyes back and concentrated on his breathing again. He supposed he would find out what his kidnappers knew, and didn't know, before long. But he wondered now who else knew he had been taken captive. Did Brick know? If he did, nothing here on God's green planet would keep his Army Ranger brother from coming after him.

For a moment Phil Paxton allowed himself to slip into a comforting fantasy of Brick Paxton blasting away with a machine gun before kicking in the door to his cell. Brick then shot off the padlock that secured the chain around his waist— Phil didn't know exactly how he did that without killing *him* in the process, but this was a fantasy after all, and he could take it any place he wanted.

He was jerked out of the daydream, however, when the door suddenly opened for real.

The brighter light that entered the cell almost blinded Phil Paxton. But he was able to make out the forms of two men in traditional Islamic robes and headgear dragging another unconscious man into the room. Rifles were slung over the men's shoulders. Phil couldn't remember what such rifles were called but he knew they were Russian. Brick would know. And Brick would know how to use one. For a moment, every fiber in Phil Paxton's body wanted to see Brick standing in front of him with just such a rifle, filling these bastards in the robes full of bullet holes.

Phil watched helplessly as the man being dragged was thrown facedown on the floor, then rolled up into a sitting position next to him. Phil kept his eyes almost closed, praying that his abductors wouldn't notice he was awake as another set of handcuffs and another waist chain were applied to the new hostage. Then the men in the white robes left without speaking and the door creaked closed again. A second later, Phil head the sound of a lock sliding into place.

Phil turned to look at the man next to him. He was young— maybe midtwenties—and had obviously been drugged just like Phil had. Perhaps when he awakened, he would have some bit of information to add to what Phil Paxton already knew. Something that might help them escape.

Until then, Phil would be alone with the two most terrifying nightmare possibilities he could dream up. The second-to-worst possibility was that he would be killed.

The *worst* was that he'd first be forced into responsibility for the deaths of hundreds, thousands or perhaps even hundred of thousands of innocent men, women and children.

CABS LINED THE STREET outside the American Embassy in Amsterdam. Bolan and Paxton took the one nearest the curb as they walked back out through the gate and nodded goodbye to the two U.S. Marines against the wall. The two men saluted, then stood back at attention without a word.

Their driver huffed and puffed as he helped them lift their luggage into the trunk of the vehicle, looking up at Bolan in wonderment at the weight of some of the bags. Bolan smiled at the man but offered no explanation.

Behind the wheel, with his two customers seated in the back, the driver said, "Where to?" in almost unaccented English.

"The Hotel Amstel," Bolan told him.

The driver didn't bat an eye at the name of one of the top hotels in the world. He was obviously used to taking visiting American dignitaries from the embassy to the Amstel, and he turned the key and started the ignition.

Bolan sat back against the seat as they pulled away from the curb. Amsterdam was one of the most colorful cities in the world, and he watched through the window as they passed seventeenth-century seven-gabled houses, historic churches and elaborate stone towers. The site was actually an inland port that boasted fifty canals and more than six hundred spectacular bridges. Two of the more renowned sites were the Rembrandt House, where the famous painter had lived from 1639 to 1658, and the home where Anne Frank and her family had hidden behind a secret passageway during the Nazi occupation.

It was early winter and despite himself the Executioner

allowed images of tulips, for which Holland was famous, slip into his mind. Along the streets and sidewalks, he imagined baskets of flowers hanging from the eves of houses, office complexes and other buildings.

He sat back against the seat, pondering this cosmopolitan city. Amsterdam was no better or worse than any other midsized city. Hidden behind the freshly scrubbed and smiling faces he saw as the cab raced down the streets was the same dirty underbelly found in all large centers of population. Behind the clean streets were the back alleys filled with drugs, prostitution, murder and mayhem.

And, of course, *terrorism.*

THE CABDRIVER PULLED UP in front of the Amstel Hotel, and Bolan and Paxton both got out of the backseat before the cabdriver or bellman had a chance to open their doors.

The cabdriver opened the trunk, and then an almost humorous competition ensued between the two men to see who could pull out the most bags in the shortest period of time. By the time it was over, a second bellman had come down a concrete ramp with a rolling luggage rack, and all three began piling Bolan's and Paxton's bags onto the glistening stainless-steel bars.

The Executioner paid the driver, adding a tip sufficient enough to bring a smile back to the man's face. Then he and Paxton followed the blond bellman up the steps to the Amstel's front doors. Bolan didn't like letting their luggage out of his own control, but he could see no way around it at this point. Besides, he reminded himself, each suitcase that contained "sensitive" items was secured by a sturdy padlock. There was no reason for the cabdriver, the blond bellman or the other uniformed man who had brought the cart down the ramp to suspect their luggage contained anything more lethal than adding machines and laptops.

Once inside the lobby, the blond bellman escorted them past a grand staircase and into the Amstel Mirror Room lounge. The walls were, as the name of the room suggested, covered in reflective glass, and men and women in tuxedos, white ties and tails, and the most elegant of evening dresses were using the mirrors to their fullest, showing off their finery.

"I gotta tell ya," Brick Paxton whispered out of the side of his mouth, "this beats the hell out of being covered in talcum-powder sand all day and taking a bath with baby wipes in Iraq."

Bolan just nodded as the bellman ushered them to the front check-in desk, then stepped back and bowed. "Mr. Cooper and Mr. McBride," he said, "Pietre is already taking your luggage to your suite." His smile widened as he stood motionless in that practiced way that bellmen at finer hotels all over the world developed. It was Bolan's cue for another tip, so he reached into his pocket once more.

Again, the man who had helped them seemed thoroughly satisfied.

An older concierge in a tasteful black suit appeared at their side. "If you would, sirs," he said with a sweeping gesture. "I will show you to your suite." Without waiting for an answer, he strode off, leading them toward a bank of elevators at the end of a short hall.

Bolan smiled behind the man's back. Top hotel officials had their moves down as well as any good counterterrorist team, he reminded himself. Just as many of them as possible got in on every act so everyone could receive a tip.

A few minutes later they were on the fourteenth floor and heading down the thick carpeted hall. The door to suite 14307 was already open, and the man the blond bellman had called Pietre was just finishing unloading their bags.

The concierge opened the curtains and let in the lights of the city. It was a beautiful view, and had the Executioner been in Amsterdam for pleasure rather than to locate and rescue a nuclear scientist being held by terrorists, he was certain he would have appreciated it. As it was, he simply reached into his pocket, pulled out enough money for two more tips and said goodbye to the concierge and the bellman with the luggage rack.

As soon as the two men had gone, Bolan and Paxton carried the suitcases containing their clothing into separate bedrooms, then met back in the living room and took seats on facing wooden love seats. The Executioner glanced around quickly. The way they had come in was also the only way out. He didn't like that. But there was little he could do about it. The fact that the suite itself was as elegantly furnished as the Amstel's downstairs areas made little impression on him one way or another. He had slept in beds built for kings. And he had slept without a blanket or pillow in the same sands of Iraq Paxton had mentioned earlier. He couldn't have cared less about luxury.

He was here to do a job, to save a man's life. The life of a man more than capable of building a nuclear bomb.

By doing so, Bolan would save the lives of countless others.

The Executioner leaned down and pulled his equipment bags to the front of the love seat. After opening all of the padlocks on his luggage, Bolan unzipped the innocuous-looking suitcase nearest to him and pulled out a custom-made Kydex and ballistic nylon shoulder holster. Inside the Kydex was his Beretta 93-R, the long sound suppressor already threaded onto the 9 mm barrel. The pistol came out of the holster with a clicking sound, and the Executioner pointed it toward the carpet as he pulled the slide back far enough to see the gleaming brass cartridge casing already chambered. Letting the slide fall back forward, he pressed the ejection button on the side of the weapon and pulled out the magazine.

It, too, was filled with RBCD Performance Plus ammunition. The special subsonic rounds stayed just under the sound barrier, assisting the sound suppressor in keeping each 9 mm bullet as quiet as possible. And the bullets themselves, round nosed rather than hollowpoints, were total fragmentation rounds that penetrated solid material like a machinist's drill but exploded as soon as they hit anything water based.

Like a human body.

Satisfied that the pistol had not been tampered with since he'd handed it over to Brognola to secrete in the diplomatic pouch, Bolan reholstered the weapon and slid his arms into the shoulder rig. Next he checked the two spare 9 mm magazines in the Kydex carrier under his right arm. They, too, were filled.

Finally Bolan turned his attention to the Kydex sheath mounted under the magazine carrier. Extending just below the spare 9 mm boxes was a Ka-bar fighting knife.

Bolan drew the knife from its sheath. Slowly he rolled up the sleeve of his white shirt and shaved a short section of hair off his arm. The weapon was razor-sharp, and ready.

Across from Bolan, the Army Ranger pulled out a shoulder rig not dissimilar to Bolan's own. Constructed of the same hard plastic Kydex and black ballistic nylon, the only differences were that the shoulder system was equipped with two holsters rather than one. And in those holsters, Bolan saw a matched pair of black-parkerized Colt Commander .45s.

As Paxton began his own weapons check, Bolan turned back to the suitcase at his feet. The next item to appear in his hands had become something of a trademark for the Executioner. The .44 magnum Desert Eagle was a *huge* pistol that had been developed more for hunting and long-range silhouette shooting than combat. And, indeed, it would have proved to be a poor choice as a fighting pistol to most men. But Bolan was not most men, and he had the hand size required to manipulate the safety and other features of the big gun, and the strength to handle the massive recoil the way most men would handle a .22.

Again, he checked both the chamber and magazine in the Desert Eagle. Then the pair of extra magazines. Satisfied, he stood and slid the holster through his belt, letting it come to rest on his right hip. He clipped the magazine carrier on his opposite side, just behind where the Beretta's sound suppressor hung. He watched Paxton slide into his double .45 rig, then reach down into his bag and pull out a short dagger. The blade was invisible inside a brown Kydex sheath, but the handle had been made from some strange material that was an off-white—almost yellow—color with darker brown slots running from pommel to hilt.

Bolan slipped back into his coat, covering his guns and knife.

"Your knife handle," Bolan said, his eyes on the strange-looking blade now clipped to Paxton's belt on the side. "The grip. Cactus?"

The Army Ranger nodded. He drew the knife in a reverse grip and extended it cactus-end first.

"The light cactus keeps the weight down," Paxton said. "Besides that, it has another special meaning to me."

Bolan looked up from the dagger, curious.

"It was a birthday gift from Phil. He had it made for me from some guy in Texas."

Bolan nodded his understanding as he examined the double-edged weapon, noting the deep Damascus whorl patterns on both sides. The blade was approximately four inches long, and the whole thing couldn't have weighed more than a few ounces. He handed it back.

"What have we got as far as bigger stuff goes?" Paxton asked as he, too, now stood to put his jacket back on.

Bolan took a step away from the love seat and lifted a

larger, heavier bag. Carrying it to the coffee table in the middle of the living room, he set it on top and unzipped it. Reaching inside, he pulled out a long, odd-looking pistol with a huge tubular drum magazine attached to the top.

"A Calico?" Paxton said, recognizing the weapon immediately.

Bolan nodded. "Two of them. One 50-round drum for each, and a 100-round backup."

"Good weapons," Paxton said. "But how are we supposed to carry them?"

The Executioner dug deeper into the bag and came out with another set of ballistic nylon straps.

"Ah," Paxton said, nodding. "DeSantis rigs?"

The Executioner nodded again. "You've used this setup before?"

"Once," Paxton came back. "You mount the 50-rounder on the gun. The 100-round drum balances it out on your other side. Both are secured to the straps with Velcro but the gun itself hangs on your strong side instead of in a cross-draw position. You can fire with it still on the strap."

"You've got the picture," said the Executioner. "And these rigs will fit right over the other shoulder holsters if we need them to. The only problem is we'll need longer and heavier coats to conceal them. So for now, we'll repack them and stick them under the bed."

Paxton nodded his understanding. "Okay," he said. "What's on the paper that bureaucratic burnout Young gave you?" he asked.

Bolan reached into his pocket and pulled out the crumpled scrap of paper. "The name of a snitch," he said. "And how to contact him."

"He can lead us to my brother?" Paxton said, his voice suddenly tight.

"Maybe," Bolan said. "Although I've never found things to work out quite that easily."

"But he can get us started?"

"He can get us started," Bolan agreed.

3

A rental BMW, arranged by Barbara Price, was waiting downstairs for Bolan and Paxton when they got off the elevator. The concierge handed them the keys and gave them directions to the parking lot. For his trouble, he got yet another tip from Bolan.

"You ever think we might be in the wrong business?" Paxton asked as they left the hotel and crossed the parking lot where the vehicle waited.

"How do you mean?"

"These guys," Paxton said, glancing back over his shoulder in the direction from which they'd come. "Every time you turn around, they've got their hands out and somebody's shoving money in them."

Bolan chuckled. "If we were after money," he said, "we'd have chosen different paths a long time ago."

By now they had spotted the BMW. Bolan thumbed the button on the remote control to unlock the driver's door, opened it, then pushed the button again to give Paxton access to the passenger's seat.

As both men slid inside the vehicle, Paxton said, "Ever wonder why we do it?"

"You're doing it to find your brother," Bolan said as he started the engine. "What better reason do you need than that?"

"I mean, the rest of the time," said Paxton. "Ever wonder why we risk our lives to help people we don't even know?"

"We help them because we *can*," Bolan said. "And because not very many other men have the abilities we do."

Slowly Brick Paxton nodded his understanding. But an introspective frown stayed on his face. And a trancelike look remained in his eyes.

Bolan pulled the BMW out of the parking lot and drove just below the posted speed limit through the city. Soon, they were on a highway leading out of Amsterdam. It was not until then that Paxton spoke again. "I didn't like you at first," he suddenly said.

The Executioner didn't answer.

Paxton turned slightly toward Bolan in his seat. "I'm more used to giving orders than taking them," he said. "Except from officers, of course. And I didn't have you pegged as an officer."

"Then you had me pegged right," Bolan said as multicolored fields of flowers, windmills and other sights flashed by.

"But you served, didn't you." It was a statement rather than a question.

Bolan answered anyway. "I served," he said. "NCO."

"Rangers?" This time Paxton's tone did invite an answer.

"Special Forces," Bolan said.

"Ah." Paxton nodded. "The Green Beanies." He paused. "Okay. You guys were all right, I guess." The last sentence was said with the feigned condescension all special squads exhibit toward one another.

Such rivalry between Rangers, Green Berets, Navy SEAL, and other such units was expected and both men chuckled now. Bolan looked up to see a sign that read *Marken 10K.*

"Anyway," Paxton went on, "I thought you were just another damn bureaucrat afraid to bend the rules. You see, I don't care *what* I have to do to get my brother back safely."

"I bend the rules when I have to in order to get the job done," Bolan replied. "Other times, I *shatter* them." He saw an egg-shaped lump form in Paxton's throat as the man swallowed.

"Well," the Ranger said. "Just in case I get killed before I get a chance to say this, *thanks*. I appreciate your help in finding my brother.

"Both of our parents were killed in a car accident my senior year in high school," Paxton went on. "I was seventeen at the time. Phil was sixteen. We didn't have any other relatives."

Bolan glanced quickly toward the other man, frowned, then turned back to the highway. "I'm surprised the court didn't put you both in foster homes," he said.

"I'm sure they would have if they'd known about our situation." Paxton chuckled. "But we both kept quiet and slipped through the cracks. That's probably when I first began to develop such *great respect* for bureaucracy." His last sentence dripped with sarcasm. But when he went on, his voice was lighter again. "The folks had the house already paid off, and Phil and I both got jobs after school to pay the utilities and other bills. We didn't do any high-rolling. But we got by."

Ahead, the Executioner saw an arrow pointing out the exit to Marken. He let up slightly on the accelerator.

"Anyway, when I graduated I got a full-time job working construction," Paxton continued. "Stayed home until Phil hit eighteen and they couldn't take him away if they found out. He'd always shown a great interest and aptitude in all the sciences, and he wanted to go to college. I didn't. So I went off into the Army and he headed for Yale on a scholarship."

Bolan slowed even more as he took the exit, nodding for Paxton to continue if he chose to do so.

The Army Ranger did. "So Phil and I are closer than most brothers, I think. Sort of like the guys you go through a war with. It's like we survived a different kind of war together, and neither of us could have pulled it off without the other one."

Bolan knew what the man meant, and said so.

"Maybe I am too close to this whole thing to be objective." Paxton paused again momentarily, then said, "But I'm going through with it anyway. I'll leave it up to you to tell me if I'm letting my emotions get in the way of my thinking."

"Don't worry," Bolan said. "I will."

Paxton laughed. "Now why doesn't that surprise me?" he asked rhetorically. "Anyway, that's enough on the subject." He closed his mouth.

Bolan took a left off the exit road and entered the small fishing village of Marken. He had seen windmills in Amsterdam and along the road during the drive, but Marken itself was like a Disneyland version of Holland. Everywhere he looked now he saw women dressed in pinafores. Most obvious of all were the Dutch clogs, the wooden shoes that had captured the imagination of the entire world. It seemed that there was a store selling them on every corner.

"Damn," Paxton said, sitting forward in his seat. "I didn't know people really wore those things anymore."

"They don't in the cities," the Executioner said. "But out here, yeah. Particularly since it's the town's leading industry besides fishing."

"I'd think they'd hurt your feet," Paxton said.

"Well," the Executioner came back as he drove slowly on down the street. "You can find out for yourself if you're really interested." He slowed the BMW, then pulled into an empty parking space under a sign which read *Klompenmaart*. "We're meeting the informant inside here. It's the shop of a custom wooden shoemaker."

Bolan killed the engine and both men got out. The *Klompenmaart* was roughly halfway down a small shopping strip, and from somewhere in one of the stores classical music came piping out. On the sidewalk, men, women and children all walked expertly past in the wooden shoes, chattering happily away in Dutch.

Paxton was taking it all in. "If they hurt your feet, these folks must have gotten used to it," he said. "I don't see anybody limping."

A light snowfall had begun a few minutes earlier, and now huge flakes fell from the sky but melted as soon as they hit the pavement in front of the shop. The Executioner led the way beneath the sign toward the front entrance. A bell chimed as he twisted the knob and opened the door. Stepping to the side, he let Paxton enter first, then stepped in and stopped just past the door, letting it close behind him. The shelves along the walls were lined with row after row of wooden shoes. Some were simple and plain. Others were elaborately painted with pastoral scenes of farmhouses, windmills, cattle and sheep. They were arranged according to size with the smallest just to the left of the door. The sizes grew larger as the Executioner's eyes moved clockwise around the room. Small, handwritten white stickers attached to the shelves gave European, British and American sizes, and told Bolan that a great deal of the wooden shoe trade had to come from tourists.

He suspected there were as many wooden shoes in the U.S. being used as flower pots as there were being worn in all of Holland.

Just in front of the back wall—the only wall on which the shoes were not displayed—was a large workbench. Scattered across the scarred wooden top was a variety of whittling knives and scoop-shaped instruments, and standing behind it was an elderly man working busily on what was still, at this stage, more a block of wood than a shoe. Reading "half glasses" threatened to fall off the end of his nose as he hacked away at the wood with a large cleaver.

In response to the bell that had rung when Bolan and Paxton entered the shop, the shoemaker now looked up over the lenses. He continued chopping, not even speaking as the two men approached the bench. But as they stopped, before either Bolan or Paxton had a chance to say anything, he whispered in a heavy Dutch accent, "Cooper and McBride?"

Bolan nodded.

The wooden shoemaker indicated a doorway behind him and to the right with a twist of his neck. A worn and dirty curtain was all that separated the shop from whatever stood behind it. Bolan brushed the curtain to the side and entered what appeared to be a small back storage room. Paxton followed.

Neither man was surprised to see the dark-skinned Arab sitting on a folding chair at a card table in the corner. After all, the name on the scrap of paper Felix Young had given them was Abdul Hussan. The informant was dressed in Western garb, wearing khaki slacks and a blue blazer. On his head, however, was a tightly wrapped and spotless white turban.

What did surprise Bolan, however, was the other man seated at the table next to the informant.

Felix Young.

THE EXECUTIONER WAS the first to walk forward. "What are *you* doing here, Young?" he demanded in a quiet yet authoritative voice.

Felix Young squirmed in his seat. "Hey," he said. "I'm not any happier about this than you are. But I got orders from above to find out who you were, what you were doing here and why the—" He stopped in midsentence, glanced at the man next to him with a furtive expression on his face, then rephrased what he was about to say. "I'm supposed to find out why *we* were cut out of the loop."

Bolan stared at the man with a mixture of disgust and pity. Young had carefully avoided using the term CIA. Did that mean he actually thought this informant hadn't figured out who he was doing business with? Or was Young afraid that actually uttering the letters *C, I,* and *A* out loud in this deserted little back room would somehow cause America's intelligence efforts the world over to collapse?

Bolan shook his head and stared Young in the eye. "Who gave you such orders?" he asked the little man.

Young's chest puffed out slightly. "They came all the way from my *director,*" he said importantly. The inference was that the man he knew as Cooper could not possibly go over such a head and get the orders withdrawn.

Bolan glanced to Paxton, who grinned back at him. Then, pulling his small cell phone from his pocket, Bolan tapped in a number known only to a handful of men the world over. He waited while his cell was bounced to three different dummy numbers on three different continents, pushed in a code that activated a scrambling device in case anyone could still tap into the call, then waited while the number rang.

The phone was picked up on the second ring. Instead of saying "Oval Office" as she might have if the call had come through on one of the other lines, the female voice that answered said simply, "Yes, this is Mary."

Bolan recited a ten-digit code number that the President's personal secretary compared to a list to ensure the number had not been dialed by mistake. Evidently satisfied, she finally said, "I'll ring you through."

The next voice Bolan heard was that of the President of the United States. "Hello, Mr. Cooper," the Man said. He was aware of the Executioner's several aliases, and which one was being used on this mission. After all, the orders for the mission had come from that very office in the first place.

"I've encountered a small problem I'd like you to deal with if you would, sir," Bolan said into the cell phone. "We've got a man on station here who seems to have been given orders by his director to get in my way."

"Pass the phone to him," the President said sharply.

Bolan handed Young the telephone. The CIA man frowned in confusion, wondering who was on the other end, and who this man calling himself Cooper might think could override orders that came straight from the director of the Central Intelligence Agency.

"Yes?" Young said into the instrument. A second later, his face went white. "Yes, sir. Yes, sir, I recognize the voice. No, sir. No problem. Consider me gone as soon as you hang up." There was a brief pause while Young listened again. As he did, his ears turned red, standing out even bolder against his pasty face. "No, sir," he said again. "My lips are sealed."

Felix Young's hand was trembling when he handed the cell phone back to the Executioner.

Bolan held the tiny instrument to his ear once more. "Thank you, sir," he said simply.

"I'll give the man's director a call," the President said in the same crisp voice Bolan suspected he had used with Young. "He was ordered to stay out of this already. Perhaps I wasn't quite stern enough when I spoke with him before." The President sighed, as if this was only one of a hundred or so such problems that would fill his day. "I'll make certain he understands fully when I speak with him this time."

Bolan chuckled, knowing the next call to CIA headquarters in Langley would probably be in a tone far beyond what could be described as stern. "Thank you, sir," he said, then folded the cell phone closed to end the call.

Felix Young had already risen to his feet and started toward the curtain in the doorway. Bolan reached out and grabbed his arm.

The smaller man flinched. "Hey," he said. "I'm *going*."

"*Stay* gone," Bolan ordered. "I don't want to see your face again the rest of the time we're here."

In what looked like a rare moment of firmness and conviction, Young jerked his arm away. "Don't worry," he said in a voice that came close to cracking. "I don't want to see *you*, either." Without another word, the man stomped on out of the shoe shop's back room.

Bolan took a seat at the table across from Abdul Hassan, and Paxton dropped down into one of the other chairs. The expression on the informant's face reflected amusement at the way Young had been treated.

Before Bolan could speak, he said, "The man is an idiot," in only slightly accented English.

"No argument here," Brick Paxton agreed.

Hassan smile widened. "What am I to call you?" he asked.

"I'm Matt Cooper," Bolan said. "This is John McBride."

The Arab held out his hand and shook both Bolan's and Paxton's firmly. "You have been told about me?" he asked. "And why I am willing to work with you?"

Bolan nodded. "We were told that you were a moderate Muslim who doesn't believe in terrorism," he said. "But still a guy who has some pretty decent contacts that might eventually lead us to Phil Paxton."

Hassan nodded. "Perhaps," he said. "We can only hope, and pray that Allah will grant us this wish." He paused a moment, then went on. "Murder, kidnapping—every form of terrorism gives all Muslims a bad name. *That* is why I have tried to help men like you. And why working with men like Young has been so frustrating."

"He strikes me as a burnout who can't wait for retirement," Paxton said in a tone of total disgust.

"That is exactly what he is," Hassan said, nodding his finely chiseled Arabic features. "New England. I have accomplished absolutely nothing during the time I have worked with the man."

"We're about to change all that," Bolan said.

"You are an answer to the prayers I have offered to Allah."

"Yeah, maybe," Paxton said. He didn't sound convinced.

Bolan had already become impressed with Hassan's confidence. It was clear that he was cut from a completely different cloth than his CIA handler, and that if anyone could get them to Paxton's younger brother it was him. "Have you come up with any place to start yet?" he asked the informant.

Hassan shrugged. "As you might guess, *rumors* abound in cases such as this. I would suggest that we begin with the most likely places where we might hear the truth and start checking them out."

Bolan nodded. Without more definite intelligence, it was the only path open to them. He purposely kept a frown off his face as he tried to decide how he should phrase his next question to Abdul Mohammed. Even though his instincts told him the man could be trusted, it could be dangerous to share any more information with him than was absolutely necessary to the mission.

Hassan was going to be trying to penetrate some of the most dangerous terrorist cells on the planet and if he became suspect, he might be tortured into telling all he knew. It was why Bolan had not told him that the man he now knew as McBride was actually Phil Paxton's brother. And why he didn't want his next question to give away any inkling of the fact that Phil Paxton was a nuclear scientist.

"Tell me," he said casually. "Do you have any idea how many other hostages are being held by the group who has this…" He let his voice trail off and frowned, as if trying to remember the specific name of the man they were looking for. It was more of the ruse to keep Hassan from knowing just how important the younger Paxton really was.

In the chair next to him, Brick Paxton picked up on what the Executioner was doing. "Paxton was the name we got, wasn't it?" he said. "Phil Paxton?"

Bolan nodded. "Yeah," he said. "That's right." Looking back to their informant, he said, "Any idea why they picked him or any of the others?"

The Arab shook his head. "No, but several Americans have disappeared in the last couple of days. My guess is that they are simply taken at random. Their crime is simply being American. All terrorist groups know that American hostages make worldwide news, and I suspect this Phil Paxton was simply in the wrong place at the wrong time."

Bolan studied Abdul Hassan's face. If the Arab knew more than that, he was hiding it well. But the question hadn't passed by the informant completely, either. "The question in my mind, however," he said, looking the Executioner in the eye, "is why America would send two specialists to look for this particular man." He glanced from Bolan to Paxton, then back again. "Two men who obviously outrank the local CIA chief of station, and can even override orders from their *director*. *That* has never happened before."

Bolan nodded, still keeping his face noncommittal. Their very presence had made a smart man like Hassan suspect that there was something very special about Phil Paxton. But with any luck, he suspected he could mislead the man and quell his suspicions. "That's a legitimate question," he stated in a neutral tone, "and I'm sure you'll understand if I can't explain all of what's going on to you, and why I even have to be vague about what I *can* say." He stopped talking long enough to draw another breath, then went on. "You're aware, of course, of Homeland Security?"

"Of course." Hassan sat back against his chair and crossed his legs. "The whole world knows of it."

"Let's just say we're with an agency that can—like you said—override the CIA when we need to," Bolan said. "And that policies and priorities change sometimes. Right now there's a real emphasis on freeing American hostages the world over."

Paxton had caught onto what Bolan was doing again and stepped in to assist him. "There are teams like us all over the Middle East and other places," the Army Ranger said. "Anywhere where even one American has been kidnapped by Islamic fundamentalists." He paused a second, glanced at the Executioner, who nodded for him to go on, then said, "We know *some* of their names. Paxton happens to be one of those."

Hassan nodded his understanding. "I do not wish to insult you, but Americans are famous for having a very short attention span. I see that a multitude of hostages suddenly being freed would not only remind your fellow countrymen that their government is still fighting the war, but might demoralize the enemy, as well."

"You've got it," Bolan said.

"I hope we are successful." Hassan nodded. "As I have already said, such terrorism reflects poorly on Islam. But it sounds very much like typical American politics, too. What is important today may not be tomorrow."

Bolan and Paxton both chuckled—but without humor.

"Politics is always a component," the Executioner said. "So

if we want to rescue these people, we have to do it while this issue is still at the top of the pile on the President's desk." If Hassan wanted to believe politics was the real reason why he and Paxton were putting so much time, effort and American money into trying to free Phil Paxton, that was fine with him.

"So," Bolan said. "Where do we start?"

"Right here in Amsterdam is as good a place as any. And better than most." The Arab paused for a second, then added, "My guess is that the hostages are here. There are plenty of Islamic areas of Amsterdam these days, which means they could be hidden in any one of them."

The Executioner had already noted that Hassan had a clear mind. "What's your best guess as to which group is behind the kidnappings?" he asked.

Hassan shrugged. "I cannot be sure. But the Hands of Allah, led by a man named Dawud A., is the first to pop into my mind."

Bolan stood up from his chair. Paxton followed his lead. "You have your own transportation?" Bolan asked. "Being seen with us by the wrong people is a pretty remote possibility. But it doesn't hurt to be careful, either."

"I have a car," the Arab said, joining the two Americans on their feet. "Where should I meet you?"

Bolan gave him the name of their hotel and room number, then turned and walked to the curtain. The other men followed.

The shoemaker had turned the block of wood into what now looked like a rough shoe by the time the three men walked back through his shop. He didn't bother looking up as they left. Whoever the man was, the CIA obviously paid him for the use of his back room as a meeting place. And to keep his mouth shut about such meetings, as well.

The Executioner stepped out of the shop, hearing the bell on the door ring once more. Once on the sidewalk again, he glanced instinctively up and down the street as he started toward the BMW.

Nothing looked any different than it had when they had entered the shop a half hour earlier. Men, women and children still clicked and clattered along in their wooden shoes, and nothing seemed out of place.

The bell sounded again as Paxton or Hassan let the door close behind him. But the musical notes were cut off suddenly but a far louder noise.

As he walked toward the BMW, the sudden discharge of fully automatic rifle fire exploded from somewhere across the street.

Bolan dived forward, hitting the sidewalk on his shoulder and rolling to the bumper of a small Toyota parked several spaces down from the BMW. More rifle fire came at him, drilling into the small economy car and shattering the windows and back windshield as the Desert Eagle leaped into his hand. Rising slightly, he saw that Paxton had drawn one of his .45 Commanders and taken cover behind a Nissan two spaces down from him.

Between the two men, Abdul Hassan squatted behind an older American-made Pontiac. The Arab was evidently unarmed. At least his hands were empty.

Another volley of fire exploded on the usually peaceful street. At the first rounds, the people on the sidewalks had frozen in place, unused to such outbreaks of violence. But as the shop windows behind them shattered into thousands of tiny fragments, shrieks, screams and gasps of horror rose over the gunfire and the men, women and children of Marken scrambled for safety.

The Executioner glanced quickly over his shoulder. There were no bodies on the sidewalk. Not even any blood. So it appeared that none of the bystanders had been hit by the bullets that had undoubtedly been meant for him and Paxton.

Or Hassan. Or all three of them.

Good. He could concentrate on eliminating the threat rather than tending to any injured innocents first.

Turning back toward the street, Bolan heard the autofire halt. In the silence that followed came the metallic sounds of an empty magazine hitting the concrete. Then came the scrape and click as another boxmag was pushed up into the weapon's receiver. More explosions sounded, and more rounds struck the vehicles in front of Bolan, Paxton and Hassan.

Bolan—his chest pressed against the front bumper of the Toyota—felt the hard vibration each time one of the rounds struck the engine block. Other rounds hit the pavement between the parked cars, causing sparks to fly up into the snowflake-speckled air.

As the steady stream of rounds continued, Bolan identified the weapon, an AK-47.

A terrorist's rifle if there ever was one.

Rising slightly, the Executioner peered up over the Toyota's hood, through the shattered glass of the windshield. All of the fire appeared to be coming from a single gunman, which didn't make sense. The only Islamic terrorists who worked alone were the suicide bombers. When such men came after you with guns, they came in packs.

Something was wrong with this picture.

The gunman with the AK-47 had obviously seen all three of them take cover. And now he appeared to be concentrating his fire more on the Pontiac behind which Hassan crouched than the vehicles in front of Bolan and Paxton. Waiting until another volley of fire was under way, the Executioner rose higher and caught his first glimpse of their adversary.

The man stood between two cars parked on the other side of the street, making no attempt to take advantage of the cover they could have provided him. He obviously did not expect his targets to fire back.

Which didn't make much sense in the Executioner's mind, either.

Looking closer, Bolan could see that the stout, dark-skinned man wore Western clothing instead of traditional Middle Eastern wear.

Unless he put a halt to the gunman's assault soon, their attacker stood a good chance of getting lucky and hitting one of them. Or at least killing one of the innocent cowering along the sidewalks amid the gunfight.

Resting the big Desert Eagle on the hood of the Toyota, Bolan lined up the front and rear sights of the big .44 Magnum pistol and deactivated the safety with his thumb. The 7.62 mm fire was still concentrated on the Pontiac as his index finger took up the slack in the trigger. But then, a split second before the trigger broke to send an RBCD fragmentation round out of the barrel to destroy the chest of the man with the AK-47, he heard Hassan scream next to him.

"Cooper, no!" the informant called out in a voice that sounded like a plea for mercy.

A second later, Hassan had leaped from behind the Pontiac and was next to the Executioner at the bumper of the Toyota.

"Don't shoot him!" he pleaded in a quieter voice. "He is my friend!"

Bolan dropped lower behind the bumper, pulling the Desert Eagle down with him, and turning to face Hassan. "Would you care to share with us why your *friend* is trying to kill us?" he asked incredulously.

"He's not trying to kill *you*," Hassan breathed. "It's me he wants."

Hassan rose slightly and yelled, "Fared! Stop this madness!"

Almost immediately, the gunfire ceased. But the heavily accented voice that came from the other side of the street was almost as loud. "I am going to kill you, Abdul!" Fared Aziz proclaimed. "Tell your friends that if they value their lives they will get up and hurry away now!"

In the distance, Bolan heard the sound of police sirens. Someone from one of the shops had called the shooting in.

He could hardly blame them.

Just the same, the sirens caused the Executioner to frown. It was a personal feud between Hassan and Aziz rather than something to do with Phil Paxton, other hostages or terrorism in general. But that didn't mean they wouldn't all end up in a Marken jail when the cops arrived. Then would come the interrogations, which would waste precious *time*.

"If he's really your friend, tell this guy to quit shooting at us and meet us at the BMW," Bolan told Hassan as the sirens grew louder. "We've got to get out of here before the cops arrive. Tell Fared we'll work out whatever's bothering him while we drive."

Abdul Hassan called out loudly, speaking in Arabic this time. Whatever he said seemed to work. He ended his short speech by returning to English. "Please, Fared!" he called out even louder. "I can explain it all! And if we do not leave now, we will all find ourselves behind the bars of the Marken jail!"

Rising up over the Toyota's bumper again, Bolan saw the man drop the partially spent magazine from the AK-47. Still holding the rifle, however, he moved out from between the cars, walking swiftly toward the BMW. As he walked, he kept the barrel of the assault weapon aimed at the ground. But then, suddenly taking note of the approaching sirens, he quickened his pace.

Bolan kept the Desert Eagle in his hand as he rose. Aziz might have dropped the magazine from the AK-47. But that didn't mean there wasn't still a round in the chamber. Grabbing Hassan by the arm, the Executioner kept the big .44 Magnum pistol in the down-ready position as he jogged toward the BMW. Behind him, he heard the sound of Paxton's hiking boots hitting the pavement—a sharp contrast from the wooden shoes that had clickety-clacked along the sidewalk only a few moments earlier.

Sliding behind the wheel, the Executioner twisted the key in the ignition and started the car. Hassan started to get in back, but Bolan called out, "No! Get in front with me. I think separating you from your *friend* sounds like a good idea."

By now Paxton had reached the vehicle. He opened the passenger side door, shoved Hassan in next to Bolan and got into the backseat. As he did, Fared Aziz entered the vehicle through the other rear door.

As he backed the car out of the parking space and started down the street, the Executioner noted that the Army Ranger kept both arms crossed across his chest, his hands inside his jacket—on the butts of his twin Colt .45 Commanders.

They were about to turn the corner when the first wailing and flashing Marken police car appeared behind them.

OBLIVIOUS TO THE GUNFIRE that had just subsided, several automobiles had turned onto the street. This provided enough distraction for the officers arriving at the scene to halt their blue-and-white patrol car. The BMW drove away unnoticed.

Looking up into the rearview mirror, Bolan saw that Paxton had already taken the AK-47 away from Aziz. He watched as the Army Ranger aimed the barrel at the floor, pulled back the bolt and jacked the chambered round out of the weapon.

"Shake him down for anything else," Bolan ordered as he

guided the BMW up the ramp toward the highway leading back to Amsterdam. "Whatever it is going on between these two, I don't want it to start up again here in the car."

Aziz resisted Paxton's frisk, grabbing the man's arms as the Army Ranger moved them toward him. Paxton withdrew his hands, stuck one back inside his jacket and came out with a .45 Commander. Resting the cold steel muzzle against Aziz's temple, he said, "This is going to go a lot easier if you don't fight me."

Slowly, Aziz nodded.

Paxton's hands moved quickly up and down the man's body. But he found nothing more deadly than a nonlocking pocket knife—a blade more suited for whittling than combat. He took the knife anyway, dropping it into the side pocket of his suit coat, then nodding at the Executioner in the mirror.

By now they were cruising along with the heavy traffic heading back into Amsterdam, and Bolan saw no signs of police pursuit. That didn't mean there wasn't any—if the cops had been told by witnesses that the men involved in the shooting had all left in the BMW, they could have radioed ahead. At any moment, any number of marked or unmarked Holland National Police units might suddenly appear. If that happened, he would have no choice but to do his best to outrun or outmaneuver them—without injuring any of the men inside the vehicles.

While the Executioner broke the laws of all lands in which he worked on a regular basis, he lived by a personal code that was on a far higher plane of morality than any laws ever would be. And that code had never allowed him to kill, or severely injure, honest cops doing their jobs.

But as they cruised along just under the speed limit, Bolan knew it was time for some answers. He glanced over his shoulder at Aziz. The Arab was dark skinned like Hassan, but the resemblance ended there. Calling him "stout" would have been a diplomatic description. While he had the sharp nose of the Middle Easterner, his cheeks puffed out almost as far as his nostrils. Heavy jowls hung from his chin, and the rest of his body appeared to be just as pudgy beneath his jeans and leather jacket. In fact the jacket had been left unzipped because the heavy belly stretching against a heather-gray T-shirt wouldn't allow for closure.

The Executioner turned his attention back to Hassan, who sat just to his side. The man was staring out the windshield, his face expressionless. But he fidgeted now and then with his hands, moving them to his face to stroke his mustache, back to fold them in his lap, then to his face again. He was clearly uncomfortable with the entire situation.

"Okay," Bolan said. "Which one of you wants to tell me what's going on before I decide to just shoot you both and be done with it?"

Hassan didn't speak. But Aziz did without hesitation. "My sister is heavy with child," he said in less-polished English than that of Hassan. "And this man—this man who claimed to be my friend—is responsible!"

Turning again, Bolan met the informant's eyes. Hassan nervously shrugged in admission.

In the backseat, Brick Paxton broke out in laughter. "I thought you Muslims didn't believe in such things," he said.

Aziz glared at the American next to him. For a moment, Hassan remained silent. Then, with another sheepish shrug, he said, "What can I say? We are but human like other people. One night Fatima and I found ourselves alone. With several bottles of wine…" He let his voice trail off, figuring the other men in the car could guess the rest of what had happened themselves.

"I thought you guys were dead set against alcohol, too," Paxton said, his laughter dropping to a low chuckle now.

"What can I say?" Hassan responded. "As I have already told you—I am a *moderate* Muslim."

Aziz snorted and was about to respond, but Paxton's warning glare silenced him.

"Okay," Bolan said, turning his attention back to the road ahead. "I want to know where that AK-47 came from."

Aziz looked surprised at the sudden change of subject. It was as if he'd forgotten the empty rifle that was now on the floor of the backseat next to Paxton. But as Bolan watched in the mirror, he saw the man's eyebrows suddenly rise in understanding. "I have a friend," he said. "Who has a friend. Who can get such guns."

The Executioner turned toward Hassan. In a voice that could not be heard in the backseat he said, "Is this guy *connected*?"

In the United States, such a question would have inquired as to whether or not the subject had a relationship with organized crime. But here, under these circumstances, Hassan knew it meant terrorists. "Not of which I am aware," he said, keeping his voice low like Bolan had done. "But this 'friend of a friend' thing. All Netherlands Arabs have terrorists at least two degrees away like that."

Bolan nodded as he slowed to meet the thickening traffic on the edge of Amsterdam. He could still see the empty AK-47 in the backseat. He frowned as an idea hit him. It was a long shot that would probably prove futile. But while he was caught up in the city's rush-hour traffic, he had nothing better to do, and trying what he had in mind couldn't hurt anything.

Reaching into his pocket, he pulled out his cell phone. A moment later, he had bounced his call off the dummy numbers, made sure the scrambler was working, and was talking to Barbara Price at Stony Man Farm. "Have the Bear check a serial number for me, will you, Barb?" he said, referring to Aaron Kurtzman, head computer wizard at Stony Man Farm.

"Sure thing," the beautiful honey-blond mission controller came back. "Firearm?"

"Uh-huh," Bolan said. "Kalashnikov." He knew Paxton had heard him, and now he reached behind him. Paxton pushed the Russian assault rifle into his hand and the Executioner brought it up and over the seat, into his lap. "Being of Soviet origin," he said. "The serial number's in Cyrillic."

"That shouldn't slow the Bear down much," Price said. "I'll buzz you through."

The Executioner heard a click in his ear as he was briefly put on hold. Then, after what seemed the right amount of time for Price to quickly condense his request, Aaron "The Bear" Kurtzman came on the line.

"Cyrillic?" was the first word out of Kurtzman's mouth.

"That's right," Bolan told him.

"Give it to me," said the computer man. "The difficult we do immediately. The impossible takes a little longer."

The Executioner chuckled as he read the serial number off the weapon.

"Hang on a second," Kurtzman said when Bolan had finished.

And a second was all it took for Stony Man Farm's computer genius to track down the rifle. "That AK was part of a shipment of a thousand that just flat disappeared about the same time the statue of Lenin came down," Kurtzman said. "The trucks transporting them disappeared, too. They're believed to have been hijacked and sold on the black market during all of the confusion caused when the union bought the dust."

Bolan took a deep breath. It was about what he'd expected to hear. It meant this rifle—and the other 999—*might* have gone directly to one of the Islamic terrorist cells that were starting up in the Netherlands. Then again, the AK-47 could have gone somewhere else.

Bolan felt his eyebrows furrow as his mind continued to

race through the almost endless possibilities at lightning speed. There was another way of looking at the situation, however, and the Executioner suspected it might have merit. Unless Abdul Hassan had a more concrete lead where they could begin their search for Brick Paxton's little brother, this "friend of a friend of Fared's" might be the best place to start.

Kurtzman had waited silently as Bolan thought. But now he rejoined the call. "Anything else you need, Striker?" he said, using the Executioner's mission code name.

"Not at the moment, Bear," Bolan said. "Thanks."

"Get back with me if I can help," Kurtzman said.

"Always," the Executioner answered.

"Okay, then," the computer expert said. "As they say the movies, 'Over and out.'"

Bolan grinned as he folded the cell phone closed and dropped it back into his pocket.

"Where are we going?" Aziz asked.

"To see a friend of yours," Bolan said simply as he continued to guide the car through congested traffic.

"Which friend?" Aziz asked. "I have many friends."

"The friend who has the other friend," the Executioner said, handing the empty AK-47 back over the seat to Paxton.

When he did, Aziz's face suddenly lit up with realization. And fear.

4

One of the things the Executioner had discovered during his brief time with Fared Aziz was that the man had learned textbook rather than conversational English. He didn't even come close to having the command of the language that Abdul Hassan possessed. Which made it possible to whisper to the CIA informant next to him in the front seat, throw in a certain amount of American slang and be relatively sure that Aziz— sitting in the back of the BMW with Brick Paxton—would not pick up on what was being said.

Bolan took advantage of that situation now as they entered Amsterdam proper. "Can we trust this dude?" he mumbled to Hassan.

Their Arab informant answered in a near whisper. "To help us track down the source of the rifle?" he asked. "Or not to keep trying to kill me for getting his sister pregnant?"

Bolan suppressed a smile. "Both," he said.

"I think his word is good about me and Fatima," the former CIA informant said. "As long as I marry her, then move away to some place where we no longer bring shame to his family." He paused a moment, then added, "Of course he cannot vouch for his brothers, however."

"How many brothers does Fatima have?" Bolan asked.

"Old enough to shoot a gun?" Hassan said. "Ah…six." He

paused, then added sheepishly, "But I am afraid my situation is even a little more complicated than that."

Bolan saw him glance into the backseat to make sure Aziz wasn't following the conversation. "How do you mean?" he whispered back to the informant.

Hassan took a long time answering. Finally he breathed, almost inaudibly, "Fatima may not be the only woman who is pregnant."

Bolan turned to look at him, keeping one eye on the road. "Are you sure of that?" he asked.

"No," Hassan said. "But another man—someone I had never seen before in my life—tried to kill me last night."

Bolan frowned. He hoped Hassan wasn't already burned before they even got this mission started. "Could the attack have come from someone learning about your connection to Felix Young?" he asked.

"Maybe." The Arab shrugged. "I have no way of knowing."

Bolan continued to drive, waiting silently. He knew more was coming.

And he was right. "Last night," Hassan muttered under his breath, "a man pulled me into a doorway as I was returning to my hotel. He tried to stab me with a knife, a type of knife that didn't stand a prayer of penetrating my heavy overcoat and all of the other cold-weather clothing I wore. I suppose it might have been a terrorist who had learned of my connection to the CIA. But his poor choice of weapons, and his even sloppier technique, spells *amateur* to me."

"To me, too," said the Executioner. He paused a moment, then said, "Tell me, Abdul. We're going to be going after *terrorists* in our search for Phil Paxton." He made sure the word was said even lower than the rest to keep Aziz from hearing it. "These are some of the deadliest men in the world, and it's going to take all of our concentration to just stay alive." He paused to let his words sink in, then finished with, "It appears you've had a fairly active love life. Are we going to have to keep dodging all the fathers and brothers you've left in your wake, too?"

Abdul Hassan's dark olive skin grayed slightly. "Honestly?" he asked.

"Of course."

"I don't know," the informant whispered. "I do not drink alcohol, or use tobacco, or violate most of the prophet's other laws, either." He stopped, drew in a deep breath, then sighed. "But the flesh of a woman—even those who are married to other men—that is my weakness. And that is my greatest sin."

Bolan shook his head and turned back to the windshield. "Well, Romeo," he said, "while you're working with me, try to keep it in your pants, will you? We've got enough to worry about without having to fight angry brothers and fathers, too."

"We should not forget the jealous husbands, either," Hassan added as if it were the most natural thing in the world to say.

The Executioner shook his head again. Every man had at least one weakness in life. But Hassan's looked as if it could create major problems during this mission. Not to mention all of the false leads it could cause that would, in turn, waste valuable time during which Phil Paxton's expertise in nuclear arms might be discovered by his captors.

"Well," the Executioner said. "I've got just one word of advice for you in the future."

"What is that?" Hassan asked.

"*Condoms,*" said Bolan. "They're a good idea these days for a lot of reasons." Before Hassan could comment, however, he went on. "Back to Fared. How about the rifle? Unless he's a complete fool, he's already pegged my partner and me as American agents of some kind. He probably thinks we're

CIA. I hate to quote someone like Felix Young, but the man was right when he said that everything gets blamed on the CIA. In any case, Fared knows we're after terrorists."

He slowed the BMW, turned off the highway and onto a ramp leading down to the city streets. "He doesn't know *which* terrorists, but neither do we at this point. We only *suspect* it was the Hands of Allah because that was the first thought to pop into your head. The real question is, will Fared keep his mouth shut about all this?"

"If he's scared enough," Hassan answered with an almost evil grin, and it was obvious to the Executioner that the man wanted to see Fared frightened out of his wits in retaliation for trying to kill him earlier.

Bolan didn't smile. It was as he'd already suspected. Hassan's personal life was going to get all messed up in this mission. And he wasn't quite sure that there was anything he could do about it. At least for now.

The Executioner turned slightly in his seat, now raising his voice to a normal tone. "Okay then, Fared," Bolan said. "How do we find this friend of yours who gave you the AK-47?"

"Actually," the same squeamish voice said. "He didn't really give it to me. He *sold* it to me."

The exasperation the Executioner had felt earlier toward the man returned. "That's pretty irrelevant," he said. Then, in a sterner voice, "I'll ask you again. Where do we find him?"

"He is a very frightening man," Aziz said. "I am afraid he would kill me if I told you. Or at least hurt me badly."

Bolan's patience was running thin. But Brick Paxton's was even thinner. "So does that mean you'd rather we killed you right now? Because that's exactly what we're going to do if you don't quit beating around the bush and start answering this man's questions." He indicated Bolan with a quick flick of the .45 in his fist.

Paxton's statement got at least part of the desired result. "He runs a student hostel here in Amsterdam," Aziz said.

Bolan could feel his anger gradually rising. It was obvious that Aziz was only going to answer direct questions in the most simple way possible. He and Paxton would have to drag every bit of information they needed out of the man, one step at a time. "Well, *where* is this student hostel?" the Executioner demanded, not even trying to hide his irritation now.

"It is on Kerkstraat," Aziz almost whined. "But I cannot take you there. He will know I am working with Americans and—"

The Executioner had reached the stop sign at the end of the highway ramp now and halted the BMW. "You know," he said. "The other offer still stands."

In the rearview mirror he saw Aziz's face contort into a frown of both wonder and discomfort. "What other offer?"

Paxton had to have read the Executioner's mind because at the same time Bolan drew the mammoth Desert Eagle, the Army Ranger shoved the Colt Commander back against Aziz's temple. Suddenly, Fared Aziz had the muzzles of two of the most powerful handguns in production pressed against his head. Either one of them could have ended his life with a twitch of the finger, splattering his brains all over the backseat of the BMW.

Paxton answered Aziz's question for Bolan. "The other offer was we put bullets in your head," he said. "That we kill you instead of your college-student-babysitter-gun-running friend. Surely you haven't forgotten that so soon, so decide whether you want your head split open with a .45 and a .44 magnum right now *for sure,* or later and *maybe.*" He smiled a smile that was anything but friendly. "The choice is yours."

Aziz swallowed so hard that he looked like a boa constrictor trying to digest an ostrich egg. "Turn left at the next corner," he said in an almost inaudible voice.

Bolan complied, then followed more of the man's directions through the crowded city until he finally made a right on Kerkstraat.

"It is at number 136," Aziz said.

Behind the Executioner, Brick Paxton snorted in disgust. "A little something for everybody, I guess," he said sarcastically.

The Executioner shared his disgust but didn't comment.

They left the porno district and moved on into an area of less titillating retail outlets. After that they came to a neighborhood of large houses. As they passed, the Executioner guessed that these had once been extravagant mansions built for wealthy Hollanders. The once-elegant residences had been broken into smaller apartments for rent. Some, it was obvious, had even been turned into the youth hostels like the one Aziz had already mentioned that his friend ran.

When they came to number 136, Bolan parked on the other side of the street and killed the engine. In the front yard he saw a sign that read *Hans Brinker Hostel.*

Young men and women, many with backpacks, came and went from both the front and several side doors to the structure.

"I can't take you to him like this," Fared Aziz whined again. "You *look* like CIA agents!"

"Well," Paxton said behind the Executioner. "Just what, exactly, do you think we can do to look like college students backpacking across Europe for the summer on Daddy's money? Get a quick face-lift, grow our hair and hang Swiss Army knives from our belts?"

"No," Aziz said, looking back and forth from Bolan to Paxton again. "But those suits…don't you have any other clothes you could wear?"

Bolan didn't bother answering. Twisting the key in the BMW's ignition, he started the vehicle again and pulled back out onto the street. Driving to the nearest gas station, he stopped in front of one of the pumps and reached into his pocket for his money clip. Pressing a number of twenty-guilder bills into Hassan's hand, he said, "Fill up the tank. We'll get changed while you watch your future brother-law-law, here. Don't let him get away." Then, glancing over the seat to Aziz, he asked, "Are you armed, Abdul?"

Hassan nodded, reached into the side pocket of his coat and pulled the bone-handle of the dagger out just far enough for the Executioner to see.

"Good," Bolan said. "If he tries to run, stick it through his heart up to the hilt."

Out of the corner of his eye, he watched Aziz's face. The man had taken the statement seriously.

Abdul Hassan nodded his understanding and dropped the dagger back out of sight. The smile on his face was wider than ever.

Bolan got out of the BMW and walked to the trunk. Paxton followed. Sticking the key into the lock, he lifted the lid and pulled out a small black nylon bag. Paxton found a bag of his own, and the two men walked toward the men's room outside the office area in their suits.

Once inside, Bolan locked the door. In silence, he unzipped his bag and began changing out of his suit into blue jeans, a black mock turtleneck sweater and a dark brown suede safari vest. Unlike so many of the safari and photojournalist vests on the market today, with their gaping armholes, this one fit tight under his armpits and hid the straps of his shoulder holster. The suede leather was also heavy enough to carry extra 9 mm and .44 Magnum magazines in the pockets without creating telltale droops. He hung the Ka-bar combat knife upside down from an inner pocket inside the vest, just in front of his Beretta.

As he stuffed his suit back into the bag, the Executioner

noted that Paxton had exchanged his slacks for a pair of heavy khaki cargo pants with large pockets on both legs. He wore a navy blue V-neck T-shirt tucked into the pants, and his double .45 shoulder rig was covered with a heavy black leather jacket.

No, Bolan thought as he caught a glimpse of both Paxton and himself in the restroom mirror, they weren't going to pass for college students on vacation. But they no longer looked like Felix Young or other American agents, either. If anything, they looked like American criminals of some sort, in Amsterdam to help arrange a drug pipeline to the U.S. or to set up some other American-Dutch criminal enterprise. And until they talked, they could just as easily be taken for Netherlanders as Yanks.

The BMW's tank was full and the bill had been paid by the time Bolan and Paxton returned to the pump. The Executioner slid back behind the wheel as Paxton resumed his seat as a guard to Fared Aziz.

As the Executioner drove away, turning back toward the Hans Brinker Hostel from which they'd just come, Aziz said, "It would be much better if I called him first. Let him get used to the idea that I am bringing two strange Americans to talk to him."

Bolan remained silent for a moment. What Aziz had just said made sense. It would be odd for two men such as Paxton and him to suddenly arrive at a youth hostel—even with an introduction by Fared Aziz. It would seem even stranger to the hostel manager when they began asking questions about an illegal assault rifle with which he had furnished the man. And those unusual circumstances were likely to make the man clam up.

The Executioner guided the BMW back down the street. Calling first wasn't such a bad idea. Unless you considered the downside which was that he didn't yet trust Fared Aziz. He still hadn't had time to place all of his trust in Hassan, for that matter, and a phone call—one that would certainly be in Arabic and have to be translated either by Hassan or in Paxton's or Bolan's own limited grasp of the language— could just as easily be a *warning* that turned into a setup to get them killed.

There were a lot of questions in the Executioner's mind, and he knew he wasn't going to find the answers until they arrived back at the hostel. But this situation was no different than any other mission he'd ever been on. There were times when you had no choice but to take risks. You figured the odds, decided how important the information you wanted was, then balanced the danger involved in getting it.

Calculated risks. They were part of every operation, and the Executioner knew he would be taking far more than his share of them every time he opened his eyes in the mornings.

Bolan reached into his vest pocket for his cell phone but Hassan beat him to it, pulling another cordless phone from the inside pocket of his blue blazer. "It *is* a good idea," he said to the Executioner, then waited for approval.

When Bolan nodded, Hassan handed the phone to Aziz. "Make the call," he told the man behind him. "Tell your friend we're American businessmen interested in opening a whole chain of hostels across Europe, and that we'll cut him in for a percentage in return for his expertise in helping set them up."

"I am not sure he will believe—" Aziz started to whine.

Brick Paxton drew his second Colt Commander and jammed both guns up under Aziz's chin. "Well, you'd better sound sincere and you'd better *hope* he believes it," the Army Ranger growled in a menacing voice. "Because if he doesn't, I'm sending you to meet Allah ahead of whatever schedule He might have had you on."

In the front seat, Hassan's smile grew so wide it looked as if his face might crack.

Aziz began punching the phone number into the cell phone with a trembling finger.

And as they neared the hostel once more, Bolan's hand moved instinctively closer to the Desert Eagle under his suede safari vest.

"YOU SAY THIS GUY'S name's Hamid?" the Executioner asked as he parked across the street from the hostel. He glanced through the window of the BMW. A heavy layer of dew—not quite sure if it should freeze into ice—covered the grass in the front yard. A wide concrete sidewalk led from the curb to the six steps that climbed to reach the porch. The porch appeared to be made of concrete, too, but had been painted a bright red, perhaps to partially compensate for the winter dreariness which surrounded it.

"Yes," Aziz said, his voice trembling slightly. "His name is Hamid."

"Hamid *what?*" Bolan demanded.

Aziz shook his head. "I do not know."

"I'm not a hundred percent sure I believe him," Paxton said. He still had one of his parkerized Colts in his hand, and now he jabbed it into Aziz's ribs. "Maybe we ought to just blow this jackenape away right now and quit wasting our time with him."

"No!" Aziz pleaded. "I have done everything you have asked of me! I cannot help it if I don't know his last name!" His voice still shook as he added, "Hamid does not know *my* last name, either."

"He knew you well enough to sell you an illegal rifle," Bolan said.

"You do not have to know someone's last name to do that," Aziz said in the quiet voice of a little girl.

The Executioner nodded. The man was, of course, right.

Many criminals operated together for years without ever knowing even one real name of their partners, let alone both. It was a simple security policy. If one got caught, the less he could tell the authorities the better.

Bolan turned his eyes away from Aziz long enough to glance at the man seated next to him in the front of the BMW. When he looked to the backseat again, he said, "Does Hamid know Abdul?"

"Not that I am aware of," Aziz choked out.

Another quick glance to the front told Bolan that Hassan was shrugging. "I do not think I have ever met the man," he said. "And I was not familiar with the hostel's—" he paused a moment and looked at the roof of the car, trying to come up with the right words in English "—*sideline business,* I guess you would call it, of selling guns." There was yet another pause but Bolan remained silent. It was obvious more was coming. Finally, Hassan said, "On the other hand, while the Islamic community in Amsterdam is one of the largest in Europe, it is *tight.* I very well may have met him somewhere, sometime. Perhaps under another name."

The Executioner drew in a deep breath and held it. The question was, should he take Hassan in with them or not? If this Hamid recognized his face in a criminally favorable manner, it could prove to be an invaluable asset. On the other hand, if the two men had had dealings in the past that weren't so gracious, it could easily block his progress in penetrating the world of the Middle Eastern terrorist operating in the Netherlands.

And there was always the third, and most dangerous, possibility—that Hamid somehow knew that Abdul Hassan had a connection to Felix Young and the CIA.

The positive aspect to the situation was that, even though Aziz had purchased his AK-47 to kill Hassan for personal reasons, it had to be assumed that there was more than just a simple illegal weapons business being run out of this hostel. And a connection to terrorism at some point was the only logical answer.

Whether it would be to the terror cell that had kidnapped Paxton's nuclear scientist brother he didn't know. But he had to start somewhere.

And this was the best starting place he had at the moment.

There was another problem with not taking Hassan with them, however. It meant Bolan would have to rely solely on his and Paxton's imperfect Arabic during the conversation inside the hostel. And the Ranger simply couldn't pick up the little nuances, body language, double-meanings and other tiny things that could completely change the true significance of what was being said.

Bolan deliberated barely a moment before concluding that his and Paxton's Arabic would have to do. He simply couldn't take the chance of burning Abdul Hassan this early in the game.

"You stay in the car, Abdul," Bolan finally said. He killed the BMW's engine but left the key in the ignition. "Take the driver's seat. Just in case we need to get out of here fast."

Now Aziz was shaking all over. "You...you are planning on trouble?" he asked in a squeaky voice.

"No, just preparing for it in case it's planning on me," the Executioner said and got out of the car. He let Aziz lead the way across the street, then stepped up next to the man halfway up the walk to the front door. "One other thing," he said in a low voice as they approached the red steps to the porch.

"Yes?" The word came out of Aziz's mouth an octave too high.

"You talk *slow* when we get inside. Slower than you did on the phone, so my partner and I can follow it."

"But if I speak *too* slowly," Aziz said, "Hamid will know something is wrong just from that."

Paxton hadn't regained any patience for the man. He stepped up behind Aziz and said, "Then you'd better find a happy medium. Because you're going to be the first man I kill if things go south."

They mounted the steps to the red porch and crossed to the front door. Bolan lifted the crescent-shaped door knocker and let it fall against a brass plate several times. A few seconds later, he was surprised to hear a female voice call out in an accent of the American Deep South. "Hold on to yer chewin' gum," the woman said. "I can't get there no quicker than I can."

A moment later the door swung open, and for a second the Executioner wondered if he'd been sent back in time. The girl standing in front of him was barefoot—and had been for a long time if the dirt on her toes was any indication. The toes, however, were all he could see of her feet because her huge bell-bottom jeans dragged the floor, covering the rest of her feet. The jeans were old, faded almost white, and held together more by different-colored patches from a variety of fabrics than the original denim. The wide leather belt that held up the pants was well below her navel in true "hip hugger" fashion, and her stretchy orange tank top stopped just below her breasts.

But her smile seemed genuine enough as she shook a long lock of blond hair away from her face and said in the same Southern accent, "Can I help you?"

Since she was obviously American and speaking English, Bolan took the lead. "Yes," he said. "We're here to see Hamid." He glanced down at Aziz to his side. "My friend called ahead a few minutes ago."

"Ah, so that was what all of the excitement was about," drawled the southern blonde. "I've been shacked up here with Hamid for almost six months and I'm learning some Arabic. But I swear, when they get to talkin' fast it comes out soundin' like one of those old Chipmunk Christmas records."

All three men smiled politely.

"By the way," said the girl, "I'm Star." She stepped back and opened the door the rest of the way, waited for them to come inside, then shut it again. Star then led them down a short hallway and past two open doors. Through the openings, the Executioner could see long rows of beds, some made, others disheveled. A few had backpacks or well-worn suitcases on them, and in a few others were young men and women, sleeping off all-night train rides or all-night parties or both.

Bolan followed Star toward the end of the hall, wondering exactly what had suddenly made him uneasy. Star had said something that immediately put him on guard, and he found that his right hand had begun scratching his chest, casually putting it within inches of the Desert Eagle under the suede safari vest.

Something was wrong. He could feel it.

But what was it?

The answer hit the Executioner just as Star reached out to open the door at the end of the hall.

"*So that was what all of the excitement was about*," the young woman had said. And then she'd inferred that Hamid was not alone—his "friends" were there with him—and they were so excited they were chattering like the Chipmunks.

So what was so exciting about a couple of American business speculators coming to check out the hostel business?

The answer was *nothing*.

Somehow, some way, and in a way that neither Paxton nor Hassan had picked up on by hearing only one side of the telephone conversation, Aziz had alerted Hamid that trouble was on its way.

It made no difference at the moment whether Hamid was connected to the Hands of Allah or whatever other terrorist cell was holding Phil Paxton. For that matter, he might not be anything more than a middleman who supplied arms to anyone who could pay his price.

Bolan suddenly knew that as soon as the office door opened, the first face Hamid and his companions saw was going to take a bullet.

Bolan reached out to grab the young woman's arm just as her hand closed around the knob. He was a split second too late. Star had already pushed open the door and said, "Hamid, the men you were expecting—" when the first round exploded from inside the hostel office.

From where he stood next to the partially opened door, the Executioner couldn't see the gunman or any of the other men in the office. But he saw the result of the shot as it struck Star in the side of the neck and threw a fistful of flesh and blood back against the wall of the hallway.

The bullet ended Star's words in midsentence. As to her life, Bolan had no time to find out.

He was too busy kicking the door the rest of the way open and drawing the Desert Eagle from under his vest.

Behind him, the Executioner could hear loud shouts and screams as the young hostel residents reacted to the gunshot. Then, as the door swung back, crashing into the wall behind it, he heard the sound of running feet.

After that, the only sounds came from firearms.

The Executioner's combat-honed mind took in the situation in a microsecond. One man stood behind a desk, his arm just then coming back down from the recoil of the round he'd fired from what looked like a Smith & Wesson 4513. The stubby-barreled pistol carried .45ACPs and, being handle heavy, had a tendency to flip back and up in the hands of all but the most well-trained shooters.

The dark-featured man behind the desk didn't fall into that category of "tactical elite." And it cost him his life.

Bolan pulled the trigger on the big .44 Magnum gun the second the barrel came in line with the shooter's head. An RBCD Performance Plus round drilled into his skull, making it explode like a watermelon smashed with a sledgehammer.

The S&W pistol fell to the desk as the man who had held it slithered out of sight to the floor.

But that was only the first of the Executioner's worries. There were four other gunners stationed strategically around the office.

Bolan dived into the room, hit the ground and rolled toward the desk—as much to give Brick Paxton room to enter the office and back him up as to avoid the return fire that now screamed his way from what seemed like every direction. As he rolled, he saw a flash of Paxton as the man raised one of his twin .45 Commanders, then brought it down hard on the top of Aziz's head.

Good, the Executioner thought as he came to a halt in a sitting position, his back against the desk. Paxton was thinking. Aziz had set them up and, while he might deserve to die, they needed him alive. At least long enough to find out how he'd tipped off Hamid, and what else he might know about the gun-running operation and any connection to the terrorists who'd taken Paxton's brother.

But Bolan had no more time to consider either Paxton, Aziz, or the wounded girl in the hallway. Out of the corner of his left eye he saw another man—this one wielding a Springfield Trophy Match .45—maneuvering around the side of the desk to get a shot at him. Jabbing the Desert Eagle across his chest, he rested his right fist against his left shoulder and fired cross-bodied.

Another totally fragmenting round drilled through the paisley tie of the man holding the Springfield. The force of the bullet tossed him back against the wall as a red mist hissed from the entry hole in his chest. He was dead before he could slam back off the wall and collapse face down on the ground.

Still facing the door, Bolan saw Brick Paxton step into the office, a Colt Commander .45 in each hand. He raised the one in his right hand just as Bolan caught a flash of light brown in his peripheral vision on his other side. The Executioner swung the Desert Eagle back to his right and pulled the trigger as soon as he felt the barrel in line with the light brown color. He and Paxton pulled their triggers at the same time.

Another of the Executioner's flesh-destroying RBCD rounds penetrated the side of the light brown sport coat being worn by a man trying to bring a huge Ruger Super Redhawk into play. Bolan's .44 Magnum slug slammed through the man's ribs and into his heart. The entire right side of the office now looked as if a sprinkle of red rain were drifting down from the ceiling.

Somewhere behind him, the Executioner heard a low moan. He had counted five men in the office, and he had downed three. The moan had to mean that Paxton had gotten a fourth. Which, in turn, meant there was one gunman still standing, somewhere behind the desk.

The Executioner took his cue from Paxton's eye movement. As soon as the Army Ranger had fired his first round, his eyes had darted far to the left. That meant that the remaining gunman had to be in the far corner of the room.

In one smooth movement, Bolan twirled on the floor, rising from his sitting position to his knees. He brought the Desert Eagle up and over the desk. As his finger moved back, taking up the trigger slack, he suddenly saw the dark-featured man's face change from a grimace of hatred to fear. His hand went limp around the Taurus PT 938 aimed toward the door, and the Executioner could see he was about to drop the gun and surrender.

"Please don't—" came out of the man's mouth, and Bolan let up on the Desert Eagle's trigger as the Taurus began to fall.

It would be good to keep this man alive. There was no telling what information they might gain from him.

But such was not to be. Brick Paxton either missed the telltale signs of surrender or didn't react to them as fast as the Executioner. A loud explosion behind Bolan told him the Ranger had fired, and he saw the .45 strike the center of the surrendering man's chest a second before the Taurus hit the floor.

"Well, shit," Bolan heard Paxton say as the roaring in their ears died down.

The Executioner rose to his feet. Screams of terror and running feet could be heard again now, coming from other parts of the hostel. In addition, police sirens wailed in the distance.

Bolan turned to face Paxton. The man was shaking his head in disgust. "He was giving up, wasn't he?" the Ranger said.

Bolan nodded.

"I should have seen it," Paxton said. "We could have used him to learn—"

Bolan broke into the sentence. "Nobody's perfect," he said. "And there's no point in worrying about it now. He might have been of help to us, and he might not have." He used the Desert Eagle to point at one of the office windows as the police sirens grew nearer. "We've got other problems at the moment. Besides, he deserved what he got even if we missed a chance to interrogate him."

Without another word, Bolan moved quickly past the Ranger and back out into the hall. He knelt next to where Star lay on the floor, examining the wound in her throat. It wasn't as bad as it could have been—the bullet had missed the arteries. But she stared at the ceiling in shock.

Bolan turned to where Aziz lay next to her on the floor. He had seen Paxton knock out the man with his pistol, and was preparing to lift the informant over his shoulder and race back to the car with him when he saw the top of the man's head.

Star had been lucky. The path taken by the bullet that struck her neck hadn't been fatal. The medics who arrived in a few minutes with the police would be able to save her.

But Fared Aziz hadn't been so fortunate. He'd caught a stray round from one of Hamid's men while unconscious on the floor. The top half of his head was gone, and the one eye he had left stared up at the ceiling, lifeless.

Bolan drew his combat knife from the inside of his vest and quickly cut the sleeve out of Aziz's jacket. Shifting back to Star, he wrapped the makeshift bandage around her neck. By the sound of the sirens, the police and ambulance would be there within a minute or so. He had no doubt they'd be able to pull her through.

"Dammit," Bolan heard Paxton say as he tightened the bandage as much as he could without cutting off Star's breath. "I'm 0 for 2, it looks like."

Bolan rose to his feet to see Paxton staring at Aziz. "It's combat," he said. "Things happen. Now, let's get out of here before we find ourselves in handcuffs."

By now the sirens could be no more than two blocks away. The Executioner led the way, sprinting down the hall toward the front door where they'd entered. A few curious—or panic frozen—hostel residents had ventured out into the hallway since the shooting had stopped. Now Bolan and Paxton had to shove them out of the way like tailbacks breaking into the open on a football field. The Executioner leaped from the bright red porch over the steps, then led the way down the sidewalk toward the BMW.

Abdul Hassan was behind the wheel and had the engine running. But his face looked as if he'd been ready to take off on his own in the next few seconds if they hadn't shown up.

Bolan grabbed the back door, opened it and Paxton dived inside the car. A second later, the Executioner had followed him and the BMW was laying rubber on the street as it took off.

Bolan climbed over the seat to the front, twisting to look out the back a second before Hassan made a left-hand turn. He saw the first police car—followed closely by an ambulance—pull up in front of the Hans Brinker Hostel.

Hassan dropped to the speed limit as soon as they were out of sight of the hostel, then turned to Bolan. "Where are we going now?" he asked.

"To our hotel," said the Executioner. "It's time to sit down, regroup and replan."

Hassan cleared his throat before he said, "I can't help noticing that there's an empty seat in the back."

"Fared took a round," Bolan said simply. "Fortunes of war."

Hassan shrugged. "It is too bad," he said. "On the other hand, I now have one less angry brother who wants to kill me."

"It sounds like there are still plenty left to get the job done," the Executioner said. "Just drive, Abdul. And keep quiet for a while."

The CIA informant nodded and continued steering the BMW.

5

To avoid being seen together any more than necessary, Hassan skipped the valet parking in front of the Hotel Amstel and pulled into an open spot on the street a block away. Then he, Bolan, and Paxton all entered through different doors and took separate elevators to the fourteenth floor. They met again at the door to room 14307, and the Executioner slid the card key into the slot, waited until the green light flashed on, then pushed the door open and stepped back.

The three men had remained silent during the drive back to the hotel. Bolan had done so in order to plan a new avenue of attack that would lead them to Phil Paxton before the young scientist was either killed or his abductors learned of his nuclear capabilities and forced him into constructing some sort of nuclear device or dirty bomb. Brick Paxton had stayed quiet in the backseat, and Bolan suspected the Ranger was mentally kicking himself both for shooting the man who had wanted to surrender and for allowing Aziz to be killed.

As far as the Executioner was concerned, he saw little chance that Hamid's man could have provided them with much, if any, useful information regarding where Phil Paxton was being held. Hamid's whole operation appeared to be more criminally driven than political, and while the men at the hostel *might* have known something about the abduction of Paxton and the other Americans, it was doubtful.

Once inside the suite, the three men took seats around the coffee table in the living room. Bolan dropped down into an overstuffed armchair. Paxton chose a recliner, and Hassan ignored the couch, instead pulling one of the straight-backed wooden chairs from the table near the kitchenette toward the group, flipping it around backward and folding his arms over the backrest.

"Okay," the Executioner said when they were all seated. "This one didn't pan out. Somehow, Fared alerted Hamid that trouble was headed his way." As he said the words, he watched Hassan out of the corner of his eye. While he didn't really believe that the informant was trying to work both sides of the fence, he still couldn't be certain. But if Abdul was dirty, he showed no signs of it now.

"But how?" Paxton asked. "I might have missed something given my limited grasp of the language, but Abdul should have caught it."

The informant shook his head. "I noticed nothing out of line, either," he said, his face a mask of truth.

Bolan continued to study the man's face for any trace of a lie, but he didn't see any. So he said, "It's not that hard to figure out. They must have had a prearranged signal of some sort which originated on Hamid's end of the line—so we couldn't hear it. It could have been anything. Something as simple as Hamid asking Aziz how the weather was and Aziz answering with something that didn't make sense. Like yes or no. No matter how good a grasp you have on a language, you can't snap to something like that if you can only hear half of a conversation."

The Executioner waited until he saw an expression of understanding on both of the other men's faces, then went on.

"But the bottom line is we're in no worse shape now than we were when we started. This lead was pretty much a fluke, anyway. It came along because of what sounds like an extremely active love life on Abdul's part, and we followed it up on the off chance it might eventually lead us to Phil Paxton." Out of the corner of his eye, Bolan was still watching for any reactions on Hassan's face, but he still didn't see any.

Hassan still thought Brick Paxton's name was McBride and still didn't know that the kidnapped American was Paxton's brother. If Hassan had figured out any of that on his own, his face didn't show that, either.

"So we start from scratch again," said the Executioner. "Give me a quick rundown on the local radical Muslim scene, Abdul. I read all of the reports. But reports are never as good as current, on-the-ground intelligence."

Hassan, still dressed in his navy blue blazer, khaki slacks and white turban, shrugged. "Well, as you know, the radicals outnumber us moderates. *Vastly* outnumber us, as a matter of fact. To be honest with you, Amsterdam—all of the Netherlands, for that matter—is a hotbed of terror. There are more terrorist groups, splinter groups and cells than anyone can count. They've even got the government officials scared silly." He paused, stood up and walked to the wet bar at the side of the room. "Anyone want anything?" he asked.

Both Bolan and Paxton declined.

Hassan found a glass in one of the cabinets, filled it at the sink, then went on. "You've heard of Theo van Gogh?"

Paxton sat forward in his seat and frowned. "You talking about Vincent van Gogh's brother?" he asked. "The brother who supported his painting when he was broke and crazy and doing things like cutting off his ear? What would *they* have to do with anything?"

Hassan smiled as he walked back to his chair. He crossed

his arms over the back and balanced the water glass on one forearm. "No, *this* Theo van Gogh was a filmmaker. He made documentaries about radical Muslim atrocities." He paused and took a drink. "He was kidnapped and murdered a few years ago."

"Where's all this leading us, Abdul?" Bolan wanted to know.

"I'm just trying to give you an idea of what you're up against here," Hassan said. "Bottom line is, even Dutch politicians who oppose the radicals have been forced into hiding. When they do go out, they travel with more bodyguards than your President. And it doesn't help that there's very little punishment when the radicals get caught, either."

"Give me an example," Bolan said.

"Okay," Hassan agreed. "Let me throw another name at you. You remember a politician named Geert Wilders?"

Bolan shook his head. "The name rings a bell somewhere, but I can't place him."

"You remember the name because the case made national news," Hassan said. "The leader of the Hands of Allah—who, as I mentioned, is known as Dawud A.—put out a contract on Wilder's life because he opposed them. Dawud got caught and convicted before Wilders could be killed." He paused to take a drink of water. "Do you want to know what his sentence was?"

"Beheading, I'd hope," Paxton said.

The Executioner remained silent. He remembered the case now, and he remembered the punishment.

"No," Hassan said. "No death sentence. He got 120 hours of community service."

"Community service?" Paxton said in astonishment. "You've *got* to be kidding."

"I only wish I was," Hassan said as he set his glass back on his arm. "The judge was scared they'd come after him next." He took another sip from the water glass. "They say crime doesn't pay. But terrorism seems to. At least here in Holland these days."

"And I thought American courts had gone soft," Paxton said, still shaking his head in disbelief.

The Executioner found all of this interesting, but he was still in a hurry to get on with the mission. "So you're saying this Dawud A. and his group might be responsible for the kidnapping?"

"It's quite possible," Hassan said. "As I have already said, they call themselves the Hands of Allah. There are always rumors that follow any kidnapping, but the majority believe it is the Hands who are behind this one."

"You have any way of finding out if it's more?" Bolan asked, leaning forward.

"I may." Hassan nodded. "There's an Arabic coffeehouse a few blocks from here. It's a strange sort of place—frequented by both moderates and fundamentalists. Sort of a neutral ground, I guess you'd call it. I have seen some of the Hands of Allah there from time to time. I can go there. At least it's a place to start."

Bolan stood. "I'm assuming that even though both radical and moderate Muslims go there, McBride and I would stick out like sore thumbs?"

Hassan smiled. "That is an expression I have never heard before," he said. "But I can take it from context." He finished his water and stood up. "Yes, you would stick out like injured thumbs. It isn't *that* neutral. I doubt you'd be harassed. Just ignored." He walked to the counter and set his empty water glass down. "I hate to ask, but do you have a little money you could advance me?"

Paxton stood up. "As far as I'm concerned," he said, "you can wait on payment until you've actually *done something*. So far, all that's happened is we've gotten some people shot because you can't keep your pants on."

Bolan could see the anger on Paxton's face, and knew where it came from. The Ranger was a professional soldier, but even professionals had their limits. Paxton wasn't so much angry with Hassan as he was with himself. He'd been a second slow in reacting to the surrendering man at the hostel, and the fact, however remote, that he'd killed off a potential source of information was still bugging him. In addition to that, he was under tremendous stress because of his brother. And to add to the stress, he'd just seen collateral damage in the form of an innocent young woman getting shot. That strain and frustration was coming out now, directed at Abdul Hassan for not leading them to Phil Paxton quicker than either he or Bolan had any right to expect.

So the Executioner changed the subject. "I'm assuming you need some more fundamental clothes to visit the coffee-house?" he asked Abdul.

"It wouldn't hurt," Hassan said. "I could go like this—there'll be other moderates there. But if I want to get closer to the crazies, especially the Hands of Allah…" He let his voice trail off.

Bolan reached in his pocket, pulled out his money clip and peeled off several bills.

"Thank you," Hassan said as he accepted them. "There's a shop along the way where I can be outfitted just fine."

Then, looking to Paxton, he smiled sadly. "Believe me," he said, "I will do everything possible to help you find this kidnap victim."

Paxton realized he'd overreacted and nodded, his face coloring slightly.

Hassan bowed slightly, then turned on his heel and disappeared through the door to the hallway.

As soon as he was gone, the Army Ranger flopped back down in his recliner. "Dammit, Cooper," he said. "I'm worthless."

"What makes you say that?" Bolan asked as he walked to where they'd left their bags earlier. He unzipped one of the heavier ones and pulled out a box of .44 magnum RBCD ammunition and another of .45-caliber Winchester Silver-Tips for Paxton.

Paxton caught the ammo box when Bolan tossed it to him. "I'm not operating at full throttle," the Ranger said. "I'm personally involved, and I'm letting it get to me."

"That's why the President had you stopped from coming here yourself," Bolan said. He drew the Desert Eagle, ejected the partially spent magazine and began filling it.

Across the coffee table from him, Paxton began his own reloading process. "I saw that guy trying to drop his gun," he said in a low voice. "I saw his face change. And at the same time, I knew we needed to talk to *anyone* who might know anything about Phil." He paused and pressed another Silver-Tip into the magazine of one of his Commanders. "And I shot the son of a bitch anyway."

Bolan nodded. "You let your emotions take over," he agreed.

The Executioner had never been without emotion himself. Ever. But he had learned to distance himself from any feelings that interfered with a job that needed to be done. Paxton would have to do the same if he was going to be useful on this mission.

"Someday, maybe," Bolan finally said, "if we have time, I'll tell you the story about how I got started in this business. But the moral to that story, I'll tell you now." He cleared his throat. "You can't hold yourself responsible for what happened to Fared. I saw you hit him over the head and, at the time, I remember thinking it was a smart move on your part. We didn't want him sneaking away during the confusion of the gunfight." He paused again to let his words sink in. "The fact that a stray round found him wasn't your fault. It was pure accident."

Paxton had opened his mouth to speak again when the Executioner suddenly held up his hand for silence. The curtains to the suite's living room were closed, blocking the high view of Amsterdam the windows provided just beyond the railed balcony outside. But he turned toward them anyway.

Had he heard something out there? Or had he just *felt* a presence of some kind? For a man with Bolan's finely honed battle instincts, it was sometimes impossible to separate the two senses, and he wasn't sure if the warning had come from his ears or his gut.

All he knew was that *someone* was outside their suite on the balcony.

Paxton had frowned as soon as the Executioner's hand went up, and it was obvious that he had not picked up on whatever it was that had tipped off Bolan. But by now the Army Ranger had learned to follow the Executioner's lead and, when he saw Bolan's sound-suppressed Beretta 93-R leap into his hand, he followed suit by drawing the custom-made cactus-handled dagger his brother had presented to him.

Perhaps Paxton's emotions *were* affecting his judgment in some ways, Bolan thought. But the man was still sharp. He had noted that the Executioner had chosen his noiseless 9 mm instead of the booming .44 Magnum and, since he possessed no suppressed firearm himself, had gone for his knife instead of one of the Colts.

Holding a finger to his lips for silence, Bolan walked quietly across the carpet toward the curtains. Pulling a corner of the cloth back ever so slightly with the suppressor at the end of the Beretta's barrel, he peeked through the opening.

There, standing almost against the glass with a state-of-the-art listening device attached to one ear by a cord, and the other end of the cord plugged into a suction-cup device attached to the glass door, stood a man in a musty brown suit partially covered by a worn black wool overcoat. Hanging from the railing of the suite directly above them was a rope ladder— the kind used for emergency fire escapes in two-story houses and that could be found in any mail-order catalog that specialized in security and safety devices.

The man had his head turned away from the Executioner, and it took Bolan a few seconds to recognize him. But as soon as he did, he reached through the curtain, flipped the lock on the door and slid the glass open.

Felix Young had a shocked look on his face as the Executioner reached up, grabbed a handful of his thinning white-brown hair and hauled the CIA man into the room. Before Young could even speak, Bolan released his grip and slapped him, open-handed, across the face.

The blow was sufficient enough to send the languid CIA station chief reeling farther into the room. Young's back struck the couch in front of the coffee table. He flipped over the table and landed on the floor.

Bolan closed the door again and locked it as Brick Paxton grabbed Young by the arm and hauled him to a sitting position on the couch. One of the razor honed edges of the Damascus blade pressed into the CIA man's throat as the Army Ranger waited for Bolan to circle the couch and take the lead once more.

"You know, Young," the Executioner said as he dropped down into his armchair and rested the Beretta in his lap. "I've got to hand it to you. You're showing a great deal more initiative than I'd have ever given you credit for after our first meeting. I'm especially surprised that a man in your physical condition would risk coming down on that rope ladder." He stared at the frightened government agent, then couldn't resist a tinge of sarcasm. "Those things are made for children to climb down from their bedroom windows in case of fire. But I'm surprised that an overweight lackluster bureaucrat—

who probably hasn't done anything more physically demanding than lifting a pencil for the past twenty years—could pull it off."

If the Executioner's insults got to the man he didn't show it. Or else he had more immediate problems to deal with. "Can...can you tell your friend to *move* his knife, please?" Young pleaded in a high-pitched voice.

Bolan nodded to Paxton, who withdrew the dagger. A thin red line was visible on Young's throat where the paper-thin edge had barely torn the skin. But Young knew that it would have taken no more than another ounce of pressure from Paxton's fingers to sever his jugular, and his eyes betrayed that fact as he watched the Army Ranger wipe the blade clean on the CIA man's overcoat before resheathing it.

"Pat him down," Bolan ordered Paxton.

The Army Ranger complied. "He's clean," he said when he'd finished. Then, with a snarl of contempt, he added, "His kind always is. They don't do anything dangerous enough to need a weapon, and they're more afraid the locals will lock them up for carrying one if they get caught."

The Executioner nodded his agreement, then turned his attention back to Young. The Beretta was still in his lap, his fist curled around the grips, his finger inside the trigger guard but away from the trigger itself. Young could have easily learned where they were staying while in Amsterdam by either paying the cabdriver who'd delivered them or making a few routine phone calls. So his first question for the CIA man was, "How'd you gain access to the suite above us, Young?"

"I rented it." Young's voice came out with a squeak. "It was open."

Bolan nodded, then said, "I thought we'd come to an understanding."

"Look," Felix Young said, his voice trembling slightly. "I

have orders from my director to find out just what you guys are up to."

"And who does your director answer to?" the Executioner asked.

"Well," Young said almost under his breath, "the President, of course."

"And who did you talk to on my cell phone who ordered you to steer clear of us, superseding your director's previous orders?" the Executioner went on.

"The President," Young whispered.

"So," said Bolan, "that pretty much demands the question, why are you still hanging around getting in our way?"

Felix Young had remained frozen in the spot where Paxton had positioned him until now. Finally, he came out of his fear-induced paralysis enough to lean forward. "You don't understand," he said. "I've only got a few months left until retirement. I talked to the director *after* I talked to the President, and he told me to stay on you anyway. He says the President doesn't ever really know what's going on and—"

Bolan broke in. "I can assure you that the President *does know* what's going on in this situation," he said. "And I can assure you of one other thing, too."

"What's that?" Young asked, his voice trembling again. He knew what was coming couldn't be good.

And he was right. "I can assure you that if I see your face even one more time while I'm here in the Netherlands—or anywhere else for that matter—I'll kill you." Before Young could respond, the Executioner suddenly rose to his feet, dropped the Beretta on the chair behind him and reached over, grabbing the CIA man by the ear. As Young squealed in agony, the Executioner dragged him back toward the sliding glass door. Unlocking and opening it with his free hand, he pulled Felix Young out onto the balcony, then used both hands to force the man's face over the guardrail.

Fourteen stories below, both Bolan and Young could see auto and pedestrian traffic. The people and vehicles looked smaller than children's toys.

"It's a long way to fall, Felix," the Executioner said. "So I'd be careful on my way back up the ladder."

"I…I…" Young stuttered, his eyes still forced to look down at the ground fourteen stories below. "I don't think I can get back up." He took a deep breath. "Not in the condition I'm in right now."

Bolan not only could see the man shaking with fear, he could feel it in his hands. And Young was probably right. If he tried to mount the rope ladder in his present state of mind, he stood a better than fifty-fifty chance of winding up on the sidewalk below.

Bolan didn't like the man, or his meddling in his and Paxton's mission. But he wasn't about to sign a death sentence for an honest if lazy CIA station chief who'd gotten caught in a turf war between his director and the President.

Of course he'd *told* Young he'd kill him the next time they met. But that had been for *effect*. It wouldn't hurt the CIA man one bit to *believe* he'd do it.

Allowing Young to stand upright again, Bolan grabbed the rope ladder, jerked it up and out and pulled the hooks off the railing outside the suite above them. Then, pushing Felix Young back through the door into the living room, he dropped the rope ladder before prodding him on toward the door to the hallway.

"What about my listening device?" the CIA man asked, his terrified voice still sounding girlish.

"We'll hang on to it for you," Bolan said. He remembered that the suction cup was still stuck to the glass door. "You won't be needing it anymore. And filling out all of the paperwork on how you lost it will give you something to do—something you're actually probably pretty good at."

With that, he opened the door to the hall, shoved Young outside, then closed the door and locked it behind him.

Paxton had followed them out onto the balcony, then back in. Now he began pacing the floor again as Bolan dropped back down into his armchair.

"What we were talking about before," the Army Ranger said. "The part about Fared getting shot while he was unconscious. That *doesn't* bother me. At least not as much as shooting the guy who was trying to surrender." He stopped walking for a moment and looked down at the floor. "There's always a chance he might have known something that would have led us to Phil."

"Yeah," said the Executioner. "There's always that chance. About one in a million, I'd say." He waved his hand toward the recliner and said, "Sit down."

Paxton returned to his recliner.

"Hamid and his friends at the hostel didn't have a thing to do with your brother," Bolan said. "They were simple, low-level *criminals*, not terrorists. I know it and you know it. So quit kicking yourself for shooting the guy."

"I've killed quite a few men in my day," Paxton said. "Shot 'em. Stabbed 'em. Killed one guy in Afghanistan by beating him over the head with a canteen. Killing them was never fun, but none of them bothered me like this."

"That's because you're confused. You're comparing apples and oranges. You think you blew some chance to find your brother. You didn't. One thing has nothing to do with the other. We just had to follow up the lead to find that out."

"Fair enough," the Ranger said. He appeared to be in the process now of pulling himself back together. "What do we do now?"

"Wait for Abdul to get back," said the Executioner. He leaned back in his chair and closed his eyes. "And I'd suggest a short nap. Once we get rolling on this, there's no telling when we might get to sleep again."

Brick Paxton nodded, then he leaned back in his recliner and closed his eyes, too.

It SEEMED LIKE ONLY SECONDS had passed when the knock on the door of suite 14307 came. But when the Executioner opened his eyes again he saw that dusk had fallen over Amsterdam. And when he looked at his watch, he saw that almost three hours had passed since Abdul Hassan had left the suite.

As he rose from his chair, he saw Paxton opening his eyes, as well. The man looked better. More calm. More peaceful. He appeared to be getting things back into perspective.

Bolan rose from the armchair and walked to the door, his hand on the grip of the sound-suppressed Beretta 93-R. He had no reason to think whoever had knocked was anyone but Hassan, but it didn't pay to take chances. Not in his business.

Besides, using Abdul Hassan as an informant had introduced other variables they had to consider. He and Brick Paxton not only had to search for the terrorists holding the Army Ranger's little brother captive but it appeared they would also have to also keep a vigilant outlook for angry male relatives of Hassan's sexual partners.

Walking silently, the Executioner stood to the side of the door. Before looking through the peephole, he drew the Beretta. Then, shrugging out of his vest, he held it by the collar and draped it down over the hole. That would darken the tiny aperture just like an eye did when a room's occupant peered out into the hallway, and make it appear to any would-be assassins that his head was right there in front of them.

More than one naive man had been killed by professional hitmen who knew that trick. They just waited until the peephole darkened, then fired their weapon of choice right through the door, into the eye looking out at them, and on into the brain.

By using his vest first, if a gunshot came, the worst it would do was put a hole in the fabric.

But nothing of that sort happened, and when Bolan finally slid back into the vest and peered through the peephole, he saw Hassan. At least the *face* told him it was Hassan. Instead of the white turban the informant had worn earlier with his blue blazer and khaki slacks, the man was now dressed in more traditional Islamic garb. He had traded the turban for a spotted *kaffiyeh* with a brown wooden *igal* holding it in place. The tail of the headdress hung down to the shoulders of his off-white robe.

The Executioner stepped back and opened the door, letting Hassan inside. As soon as the man entered, he swept the *kaffiyeh* from his head and used it to wipe sweat from his eyebrows. "It doesn't matter how cold it gets outside," were the first words out of the informant's mouth. "These things are still too damn hot for my taste."

Bolan let the door swing closed as Hassan walked past him into the room and returned to the same straight-backed wooden chair he had sat in earlier. Twisting the dead bolt, the Executioner joined him and Paxton in the living room.

The Army Ranger was fully awake now, and Bolan could see he had been right—the short nap had done the man good. His eyes were clear, and there were none of the other signs of depression and anxiety about his brother the Executioner had noted earlier.

"To use an expression I have learned from you Americans," Hassan said as he sat down and folded his arms across the back of the chair once more, "I have some good news and some bad news."

"Give us the bad news first," Paxton said.

"No one at the coffeehouse is certain who has kidnapped your man or the other Americans who have been taken recently. But the majority, at least, say it must be the work of Dawud A. and his Hands of Allah organization."

"And the good news?" Bolan asked.

"I have ingratiated myself—at least to a certain degree—into the trust of one of the more radical men I met. At least I have been invited to attend what is officially being called a Koran study session tonight at some private residence."

"You get this guy's name?" Bolan asked.

"All he told me was Ali."

"Well," Paxton said with a snort, "that narrows it down to a few million men. Sort of like meeting someone named Joe in the U.S."

Bolan felt himself frowning. "How'd you duke yourself in with Ali like that?" The possibility that Hassan had come on too strong, thereby making the man suspicious, was always there.

Hassan's smile stretched from ear to ear. "By telling them how much I hated men like *you two,* of course," he said. His expression told Bolan he had noted the concern on the Executioner's face, and he addressed it immediately. "It is always possible that I overdid it for a first meeting," he said. "But I saw no choice. Time, it appears, is an essential element in what you two have planned."

"It is," Paxton agreed. "I just hope you didn't come right out and say something stupid like 'I hate Americans and want to kill them all.'" The Army Ranger obviously had his own concerns.

Hassan looked slightly insulted. As a seasoned informant, the Arab knew as well as Bolan and Paxton that there was no better way in the world to get burned than to go in cold and start telling the enemy exactly what he wanted to hear.

Criminals and terrorists weren't stupid. And trying to forge alliances and friendships too quickly was a dead giveaway.

"Of course not," Hassan said. "I simply sat there drinking my coffee—which I can't stand, by the way, Arabic coffee, that is—and let this guy break the ice. I did a lot of nodding and threw in a few insinuations, and only toward the end did I let it slip that it would delight me if all of America disappeared beneath the ocean like Atlantis." His smile had faded at Paxton's question but now it returned. "Sort of a large-scale version of those Arabs who keep claiming they will push Israel into the sea, I suppose."

"Where is this study meeting tonight?" the Executioner asked.

Hassan turned to face him. "I don't know yet. It's very hush-hush, which tells me it's not really a Koran study group at all. It's a bunch of terrorists planning something."

Now it was Bolan's turn to frown. "This is going awfully fast," he said. "You meet this stranger and within three hours he's trusting you to participate in a terrorist strike?"

"I thought the same thing," Hassan said, nodding. "But there are other possibilities."

"Which are…?" Paxton prompted.

"Well, one is that they're a small and incompetent cell who just haven't been caught yet," Hassan replied.

"That's possible," Bolan agreed. "Even the most stupid criminals and terrorists—men who take risks for recruitment purposes that the larger groups don't have to take—sometimes slip through the cracks for a while." He cleared his throat. "But if that's the case, we can be pretty sure they aren't the ones holding Phil Paxton."

"That's the downside of that theory," Hassam agreed. "On the other hand, as you two know probably better than I do—certainly better than that do-nothing Felix Young ever figured out—working a deal like this is like climbing a ladder. You do it one rung at a time. And this group—this *rung* of the ladder, if you will—might lead us up to the next step, and eventually to whoever has the hostages."

"You said there were other possibilities as to why you were invited tonight," the Executioner said. "Inferring more than one."

"Yes, there is another," Hassan said.

Both Bolan and Paxton waited silently for whatever was to come next.

With a completely blank face, Hassan said, "There is always the chance that my new friend *does not* trust me at all, and suspects I am a spy." He paused for a breath, then went on. "Which, of course, is exactly what I am."

"So what happens tonight if that's the case?" Brick Paxton asked.

Hassan's shrug didn't quite counteract the trace of fear that now came into his eyes. "In that case," he said, "they lure me to this 'study group' and torture the hell out of me to find out what I'm really up to. And what I know about them already."

Bolan glanced at the ceiling for a moment. There was a limit to how much protection they could give Hassan under these circumstances, and the informant knew it. "Where are you supposed to meet Ali tonight?" he asked.

"Back at the same coffeehouse," Hassan answered. "He says he will drive me to the study session."

The Executioner rose from his chair and walked over to the pile of luggage still in the corner. Unzipping yet another of the bags that had come over in diplomatic pouches, he brought it back to his chair and laid it in his lap. "We'll wire you with this Nagra reel-to-reel and a transmitter," he said. "And I've got a homing device you can wear that will connect to my computer, which has been programmed in with maps of Amsterdam and the rest of the Netherlands. We should be able to follow you to wherever this meeting takes place."

"*Should* is the operative word," Hassan said. "Ali is bound to take a roundabout route, looking for tails. And they may

Get FREE BOOKS and a FREE GIFT when you play the...

LAS VEGAS GAME

Just scratch off the gold box with a coin. Then check below to see the gifts you get! →

YES! I have scratched off the gold box. Please send me my **2 FREE BOOKS** and **gift for which I qualify.** I understand that I am under no obligation to purchase any books as explained on the back of this card.

◄ DETACH AND MAIL CARD TODAY! ▼

have other surveillance vehicles following whatever vehicle we take—watching their backside, too."

"That's true," Bolan admitted. "And while McBride and I can grab some robes and headdresses similar to what you've got, if we get too close they're going to see we aren't Arab." He looked the informant squarely in the eyes. "Are you sure you want to take this chance?"

Hassan nodded without hesitation. "It's part of the job, isn't it? Taking chances?" He paused a second. "Do not read me incorrectly. I do not like working against fellow Arabs. But these men—men who murder innocent men, women and children—they are *not* my people. And in the eyes of the rest of the world—where people generalize, even if incorrectly— they give all Arabs a bad name."

"Then it's a go," Bolan said. He set the surveillance pack on the coffee table in front of him. "When are you supposed to meet this Ali guy?"

"In one hour," Hassan responded.

"Then we'd better get started," the Executioner said. He stood up, reached down into the case on the coffee table and pulled out several items, including a roll of white adhesive tape. "I hope you don't mind a little pain later." He chuckled as Hassan began to shrug out of his robes. "We don't have time for you to shave your chest."

A look of total contempt came over the informant's face. "Bah!" he almost spat. "Shaving their body hair is what some of the insane Muslims do before suicide bombings and other attacks from which they do not plan to survive." He shook his head. "It makes no sense. I mean, if you are about to be blown to bits by your own bomb, what does it matter if the tape is stuck to hair?"

The Executioner shrugged as he began plugging the wires into the small reel-to-reel Nagra unit, then secured the connections with strips of tape. Sending Hassan off into the lion's den with the Nagra, transmitter and homing device was taking a chance. There was no guarantee that his new friend—this Ali—or some of the other potential terrorists he would be meeting tonight wouldn't pat him down.

After all, Hassan would be the new kid on the block.

But as always, it was another calculated risk that needed to be taken. The Nagra would record all of the conversation picked up over its microphone so he, Hassan and Paxton could review the details later. "No, shaving their bodies doesn't make sense," he agreed. "But none of their other interpretations of the Koran do, either.

"Agreed," Hassan said as he stepped forward in his underwear now.

The Executioner had placed the Nagra in the center of Hassan's chest and was wrapping tape around the man's back. He then ran the microphone wire down Hassan's left arm, securing it first to the man's upper arm, then his forearm, with several circles of the same tape. When he was finished, the mike was roughly three inches above the informant's wrist. Far enough toward the opening in the sleeve of his robe to pick up even low conversation while still being far enough away to stay out of sight when he moved his arm.

"Turn around," the Executioner said, and Hassan complied.

The informant's back was covered almost as thickly with hair as his chest. Bolan positioned the transmitter—which would send all conversation and other sounds immediately back to the Executioner's receiver—between the man's shoulder blades and gave it the same thorough tape job as he had the recorder. Some of what came over the transmitter was likely to be inaudible. But careful analysis—later—was what the tape recorder was for. The transmitter was to alert Bolan and Paxton in the event Hassan ran into trouble and needed an immediate rescue. He ran its mike down Hassan's other arm, again wrapping it securely in place with tape.

The last electronic device the Bolan pulled out of the case was the homing device. The bug, or homer, as they were so often called, was small and could be carried or mounted just about anywhere. But if found on Hassan's person, it would be as impossible to explain away as the recorder and transmitter.

"Where do you want it?" Hassan asked.

"It is wireless, yes?" Hassan said.

The Executioner nodded his head.

Abdul pulled the spotted *kaffiyeh* from his head, turned it wrong side out and slipped the bug into an inside lining. "There," he said. "Now I can be certain that you know where I am. Unless I lose my head, of course." His laughter at his own mediocre pun was about half real and half forced from fear. Bolan knew the man's nervousness came from the fact that the joke could be taken quite literally.

Beheading their enemies was still a favored method of execution by twenty-first-century Islamic fanatics.

The Executioner pulled a laptop—customized by Aaron Kurtzman at Stony Man Farm—from a padded sleeve in the black nylon case on the coffee table and opened it up. He let the instrument warm up on its batteries, then pulled up the detailed street map of Amsterdam Kurtzman had installed. "We need to check out all of this techno-wizardry before you and Ali take off," he said as the map appeared on the screen.

By using the zoom features, he pinpointed their current position at the Hotel Amstel, then dropped back to show a two-mile radius around it. "Come here, Abdul," he said.

None of the electronic surveillance devices had been switched on yet, so Hassan's position—which would have shown up as the same as their own—didn't appear on the map. "Point out to me the location of the store where you bought your new *abaya*. That is the proper name for the robe, isn't it?"

"It is," Hassan confirmed.

"And the *kaffiyeh* and *igal*," the Executioner finished.

The Arab squinted at the screen, then finally tapped a finger a few inches away from the hotel. "Right about there," he said.

"Okay," said the Executioner. He looked at his watch, then reached into his pocket and withdrew more Dutch paper money. Shoving the bills into Hassan's hand, he said, "We've got just enough time for a dry run before you meet this new friend. I want to make sure everything's working properly before you go back to meet this guy." He paused as Hassan nodded his understanding, then went on. "So we'll watch and listen while you go back to the same store and get two more outfits like yours. One for me, the other for McBride."

"You want them *exactly* like this?" Hassan asked.

"Not exactly. But just as traditional and conservative. Something that won't draw attention to us and make people look too closely at our faces."

Hassan nodded again.

"All right," Bolan said. "Come with me to the door. I've got a few last-minute adjustments to make."

Hassan followed Bolan to the door to the hall, then stopped. When he did, the Executioner reached inside the man's garments and activated the recorder, transmitter and homing device. Then he tore off three more small strips of tape and fastened the switches with the adhesive for added insurance. That way, they couldn't accidentally be flipped off as they moved against Hassan's clothing. When Bolan activated the homing device, he heard a tiny beep from the computer on the coffee table across the room.

"Sounds like it's working," Bolan said to Abdul. "Now *hurry.* Get us our clothes, then get back here as fast as you can. You don't want to be late for this first meeting with your new friend."

Hassan hurried out into the hall.

When Bolan returned to the living room, Paxton was seated in the armchair in front of the laptop. "This is really cutting-edge stuff," he said. "We don't have anything like this in the Rangers. I just watched Abdul come out of the hotel and start down the street."

Bolan nodded. He flipped on the radio receiver and heard the street sounds coming from somewhere down the block: the unintelligible chattering of hundreds of voices on the sidewalks, a siren somewhere in the distance, one car backfiring and another screeching its tires. Then, as clear as day, he heard Hassan's voice.

"I know you can't answer me, guys," the informant said. "But I'm speaking in a normal voice just to make sure you can hear me." He waited a few seconds, then said, "Testing, one two three." Next, a stifled laugh came from the transmitter. "An old lady just saw me talking to myself and made a point of going out of her way to get around me."

"Sounds like the homer and transmitter are a go," the Executioner said. "We won't be able to check the recorder until he gets back."

"Anyway," Hassan went on. "If need be, I can always call you on my cell phone. I've still got it, and since everyone and their pet dog have them these days, it won't seem strange for me to have one." He paused. "Of course I can't do that *in front* of the study group."

Bolan turned to the luggage still stacked in the corner of the room. "Keep monitoring the screen, Paxton," he said. "And listening. Make sure everything keeps working right."

"That's affirmative," the Army Ranger said. But then, as

the Executioner unzipped yet another of the ballistic nylon cases, he said, "What are *you* going to be doing?"

"Abdul's gone to get our undercover Arab-wear ready," Bolan said. "I'm about to do the same with our battle gear."

Without another word, he pulled two pairs of tight, stretchy combat-designed coveralls known as blacksuits out of the bag and tossed them over the back of the chair where Paxton was sitting. Two nylon web belts, already festooned with holsters, extra magazine cases, and other carrying pouches came next. And then Paxton's, and his own, black leather and nylon combat boots.

The Executioner then dug down to the bottom of the bag and pulled out the two Calico 950 submachine pistols he had shown Paxton earlier. They were already set up in the shoulder slings with the 50-round 9 mm drums mounted on top of the pistols and the 100-round backups strapped in place with Velcro on the other side of the DeSantis rigs.

"You don't think we might look a little funny leaving the hotel in all this?" Paxton asked, his eyes moving from the blacksuits and web belts to the Calicos and back again.

"Not if we wear these over them," Bolan said. He opened yet another case and pulled out a pair of knee-length, beige trench coats. The coats he handed directly to Paxton.

Finally the Executioner produced two light felt hats—the kind that could be rolled up or folded into luggage but would spring back into shape the moment they were taken out. It seemed that every other man he saw these days had one on, and they were readily available from clothing stores and mail-order catalogs the world over. Most came in either the classic fedora style or the newer, trendier Australian "outback" brim, which curled up slightly on the sides like a conservative cowboy hat.

The hats Bolan had chosen, considering their destination,

however, were slightly different. Of dark green felt, they had narrow brims that curled up in the back and down in the front with a fully rounded crown. A thick rope, tied at the side, served as the hat bands.

Paxton couldn't restrain a laugh as he took his hat and set it on his head. "Alpine hats?" he said. "Should I have learned to yodel for this mission, too?"

Bolan smiled. "I think we'll be okay without you yodeling," he said. "I'm *sure* I will be."

"I take it we're going to have to be quick-change artists," the Army Ranger said. "Going from simple street tourist to Islamic terrorist to G.I. Joe in mere seconds."

"That's the idea," Bolan said.

6

As soon as Abdul Hassan had returned with their clothing, Bolan sent him out again. He and Brick Paxton had already donned their blacksuits, and now they gave their informant a two-minute head start from the room before covering their battle gear with the trench coats. To further disguise themselves, they had cut the legs off two pairs of slacks, then slipped them over their calves and knees, holding them in place with rubber bands.

That way, the only combat-oriented item of equipment visible were their boots, and black leather and nylon footwear had become so common on the streets of America and Europe that no one was likely to pay them a second glance.

The Executioner's only concern was that when they left their trench coats open, their nylon web belts—which *did* look battle ready—could be seen. And when they buttoned the coats and fastened the belts around their waists, the Calico machine pistols and 100-round backup drums were clearly visible.

But that problem had been solved by simply buttoning the loose coats and letting them fall straight toward the floor. They tucked the belts into their hand-warmer pockets, donned their alpine hats and stepped out into the hall.

The Executioner carried the laptop in a padded black nylon case that lent even more credence to the illusion that they had to be either American or European businessmen. Paxton toted a similar piece of black vinyl luggage, slightly larger. In addition to other things, it was filled with the traditional Arab clothing Hassan had purchased for them.

Bolan took note of the two other men and three women they rode down with on the elevator. Just like every place he'd ever been, the same elevator etiquette seemed to apply in Amsterdam. Everyone ignored everyone they didn't know, acting as if they were alone on the elevator. The car's passengers stared stupidly up at the numbers above the door, watching them light up, then darken again, as each floor was passed. When the doors finally slid back at the mezzanine level, the women were allowed off first. Bolan and Paxton waited for the other men to leave before stepping out.

It had been a good test, Bolan realized. The lumps in their trench coats—still partially visible under their arms—had drawn no attention.

Cutting down a side hall past a long row of rooms, the Executioner and his Army Ranger partner took a side exit outside the Amstel. They walked briskly toward the BMW, still parked on the street.

"You drive," the Executioner said to Paxton, tossing the man the car keys as they neared the vehicle.

Paxton nodded as he caught them. It was obvious he understood that Bolan wanted to concentrate on the laptop and track Hassan's movements himself once they were inside the vehicle.

The Ranger pulled out of the parking space, and Bolan directed him down the first alley they came to. After pulling into the darkness, the two men quickly discarded their coats and hats, tossing them into the backseat where they'd be readily available as soon as they were needed again. Paxton unzipped the case he'd carried down with him and tossed an *abaya* and *kaffiyeh* to the Executioner. A second later the two

American businessmen had been transformed into Arabs and they drove out of the alley in the expensive BMW, which looked as if it had been purchased with oil money.

Bolan opened the laptop and turned it on. Immediately, both men heard the homing device beep and saw that Hassan was well along on the route to the coffeehouse he'd promised to take. The Executioner zoomed the street map in until the coffeehouse was just at the edge of the screen, creating the largest picture he could as they followed their informant. He had brought the radio receiver down from the room in his coat pocket, and now he reached over the backseat, pulled it out of the coat and turned it on, as well.

Moments later, the sounds of walking, talking, laughing people met his ears. He could even make out Hassan's own footsteps as the transmitter jarred slightly each time one of the informant's feet hit the sidewalk. A few seconds later, both Bolan and Paxton heard Hassan say, "There's something going on a block ahead of me. Can't see what it is—just a bunch of flashing red lights. I'm going to cut over a block, circle around it, then resume the original route."

Bolan didn't bother to answer or even nod. The transmitter was just that—a transmitter. They could hear Hassan, but there was no way to communicate back to him unless they called him on his cell phone. And that was far too risky, considering that he might be under the counter-surveillance of the enemy at that very moment.

Traffic became more congested as they drove on, and a block later Bolan saw the flashing red lights himself. He directed Paxton to turn onto the street where Hassan had left the route, and as they did the Executioner saw the reason for the lights and congestion.

It was a simple traffic accident. No more, no less, and Hassan could have walked right past it without breaking stride. But the former CIA informant was smart. He knew the BMW would have been slowed and perhaps even brought to a standstill indefinitely.

It had been a good call on Hassan's part. Although Bolan still didn't fully trust the man, the Executioner was gaining even more respect for the man's intelligence as time went on.

As they turned right at the next corner, Bolan heard Paxton say, "I've got visual."

The Executioner looked up from the laptop to see that Hassan was now only a half a block ahead of them. "Slow down," he ordered the Ranger. "This homer's working like a charm. There's no sense in taking the risk of being spotted."

Paxton slowed down and pulled up alongside the curb for a good thirty seconds to allow Hassan to increase the distance between them. Bolan took advantage of the brief respite in monitoring the laptop to quickly scan their surroundings. Most of the stores and sidewalk stands had already closed for the evening, and on this side street the only traffic appeared to be from the drivers who, like he and Paxton, had chosen to detour around the accident.

If the group Ali represented had sent any cars to look for a tail, the Executioner couldn't see them. That either meant there was no one following them or they were damn good.

Bolan suspected the former was the case. At this point in the mission, they hadn't done much to attract the suspicions of any of the terror groups in Amsterdam. The gunfight at the hostel would probably be written off by all who heard about it as a disagreement between arms dealers, not a quest to find the hostages. His guess was that so far they'd gone unnoticed within the terrorist community in Amsterdam.

When Hassan turned right again at the next block, Paxton pulled out onto the street once more. But he continued to drive slowly, making sure that by the time they reached the corner their informant had turned left again and was back on the original, agreed-upon path. The homing device on the Executioner's laptop confirmed it, both with the blinking light and the soft beeping that signified that the unit was in motion.

By the time they had turned past the traffic accident themselves, Hassan had disappeared into the crowds along the street and sidewalks again. But Bolan could see on the screen that he was a little over two blocks ahead of them. That meant he was also just a little over two blocks from the coffeehouse. They drove on until Hassan's voice came over the receiver again.

"All right, gentlemen," he said. "I'm about a hundred feet away and heading in. If the homer's working as well as it did before, stay back. You'll be able to tell if I'm in trouble if I start speaking in English." He paused a second, then said in a slightly teasing voice, "I'll do that because I've already seen just how bad Mr. McBride's Arabic is. Over and out."

Paxton didn't take the gibe personally and even laughed. "He's right, you know," he said. "About my Arabic. But remind me to give him a ration over that 'over and out' crap. He must have heard it on TV. Who the hell actually says that?"

Bolan's only answer was a chuckle under his breath. So far, things were going smoothly. And even though the traffic accident that had altered their course had not been a significant problem, it had proved to him that Hassan could encounter the inevitable obstacles that came up during any mission and overcome them.

That was the single most important aspect of any warrior's personality. *Nothing* ever went exactly as planned. The only thing you could count on was that you could count on *nothing*. Bolan only hoped Hassan would fare as well under pressure.

Because the Executioner knew the *real fighting* hadn't even begun.

"Cruise past the coffeehouse once, just so we can see what

it looks like," Bolan told Paxton. "Then come back here somewhere and find a place to park. Like the man said, there's no reason to get too close." He tapped the laptop screen. "This thing is working great." The Executioner made a mental note to thank Kurtzman when he returned to Stony Man Farm. The computer wizard was a vital part of almost all of Bolan's missions, and this one was proving to be no exception.

The coffeehouse looked as if it had once been an industrial shop of some type. The walls and roof were made of corrugated steel, and the only thing Arabic-looking about the place was the neon sign hanging above the door.

"What's it say?" Bolan asked as they drove by.

"Don't ask me," Paxton said. "Like Abdul said, I barely *speak* the language. Can't read a word of it."

The Ranger drove two more blocks, then circled down another side street, emerging again roughly three blocks away. When he pulled in next to the curb, they could just barely see the neon sign in the distance.

On the streets around them, people came and went. Both auto and pedestrian traffic was lighter than it had been closer to the Amstel, and what speech they could hear through the closed windows was all in Arabic. They were obviously in one of the areas of Amsterdam where immigrants from the Middle East had chosen to live, and he was glad that he had sent Hassan to buy their *abaya* and *kaffiyeh*. But even so dressed, Bolan turned sideways in his seat to keep his face away from the sidewalk as families, couples and single men walked by.

In true Arabic fashion, no unescorted women came down the sidewalk. Some of the passersby might have traded their traditional clothing for more modern, European fashions. But they hadn't traded in all of their *traditions*.

Other voices, also speaking in Arabic, filled the car. Some voices were loud and raucous. Others quiet and gentle. Most were somewhere in between, and the Executioner reminded himself that people were pretty much people no matter where you went. Regardless of the color of their skin, the way they dressed or their traditions, they had the same basic goals and faced the same problems that had to be overcome in order to reach those goals. The only real difference was that different cultures went about overcoming their problems and obtaining those goals in different ways.

Bolan also reminded himself that the majority of men and women of any race, from any culture, were *good.* It was important to him that he do that periodically. Because the people with whom he dealt—from every culture—were usually the bad ones.

Still turned sideways in his seat and, using the tail of his *kaffiiyeh* to hide his face, the Executioner reminded himself that every race and culture had its share of scum. The color of the skin, what they wore and what they ate didn't change that fact. In any group of people, you'd find some who were just downright *disreputable.*

Bolan and Paxton continued to listen to the receiver as they waited.

"Are you able to make out any of it?" the Executioner finally asked Paxton after they'd been sitting there for several minutes.

"A word here and there," Paxton said. "Sometimes a phrase. I can recognize Abdul's voice when he speaks." He stopped talking for a moment and frowned at the radio. "As best as I can tell he's met up with Ali. Unless I'm really off base, it sounds like they're discussing the topic of trust."

"Whether or not Ali can trust Abdul," Bolan said.

"Yeah," Paxton confirmed. "But Abdul's holding his own pretty well. He's thrown the ball back in Ali's court several times by acting like he doesn't fully trust *him.*"

The Executioner smiled. It was one of the oldest tricks in the book, used by both undercover cops and clandestine agents. But it still worked almost every time. When someone questioned the fact that you might be "the man," you immediately accused *him* of the same thing.

"I can't even tell where this Ali guy is from," Paxton interjected a moment later. "He's got a weird sort of accent I'm not familiar with. Not Afghan or Iraqi, anyway, and I'm pretty sure it's not Iranian, either. Maybe Saudi or Kuwaiti?"

"But Abdul seems to understand him?" Bolan asked.

"Oh, yeah. It's kind of like you or me understanding an Australian or South African. It's only the colloquialisms and slang we might have to have explained."

"We'll listen to the Nagra and work on that when we meet up with Abdul again after this is over," the Executioner said.

Paxton nodded. "Uh-huh," he said. "But I've already learned one thing for sure."

"What's that?"

"It's not really some Koran study session Abdul's been invited to," said the Ranger. "Not unless they run a background check on all new members who want to read the Koran."

The dialogue between Hassan and Ali, as well as the background noises from other conversations within the coffeehouse, went on for another ten minutes or so. Bolan continued to watch the monitor screen, although the beeping and blinking dot of the homing device didn't move. The instrument was cutting-edge technology and precise, but not so precise that it could tell him anything more than the fact that Hassan was still inside the corrugated building.

Then the Executioner heard the two men's tones of voice change. And it seemed that tones—if not words—were the same in any language for certain occasions.

They were getting ready to leave.

A moment later, the blinking dot on the laptop moved slightly, back out onto the sidewalk.

"Wait for me," Bolan said, closing the laptop and handing it to the man behind the wheel. "I want visual confirmation that this Ali came out with him. And I want to see what kind of vehicle they get into."

Paxton took the computer. Then, without needing to be told, he cupped a palm over the dome light inside the BMW to keep it from glowing as Bolan opened the door.

A second later, the Executioner was walking swiftly down the street, staying behind other parked vehicles. When he was close enough to see two robed figures get into a gold Cadillac, he turned and sprinted back to where Paxton was waiting. The Ranger had already twisted the handle on the passenger's side and was leaning across the seat, holding the door open for him.

Bolan leaped inside and snatched the laptop back from Paxton. "Gold Cadillac," he said. "It's pointed this way so we'll probably have to make a U-turn. Wait until they're well past us so Ali doesn't see it in his rearview mirror."

Paxton nodded. He already had the engine running and the car in drive, ready to take off in pursuit. "A gold Caddie," he said sarcastically. "These self-righteous enemies of the Great Satan America, who hate Western technology and want to go back to living in the fourth century sure don't mind using our indulgent commercialism when it suits their own needs, do they?"

The question had been rhetorical, and there was no need to answer it. But even if it hadn't been, the Executioner wouldn't have had time. To his surprise, it was the Cadillac that made the U-turn just outside the coffeehouse. The dot on the laptop screen started moving away from them rather than toward them.

"Take off," Bolan told the Army Ranger as soon as he saw what had happened. "They're heading the other way."

Paxton drove slowly away from the curb, down the street and passed the coffeehouse once more. The Caddie was nowhere to be seen.

But that didn't worry the Executioner. So far, the homing device and accompanying software street-map program Kurtzman had installed had worked flawlessly. He could see that the gold car had turned right two blocks farther down, and he directed Paxton to do the same.

As the two cars drove away from Amsterdam's more commercial area into a residential part of the city, Bolan continued to talk the Ranger through at least a dozen twists and turns. The reason was simple enough for a child to figure out.

Ali was looking for a tail. And had they not had the homer and laptop, and been able to stay well out of sight behind the Caddie, he'd have spotted one.

But the Executioner was surprised once more when the homing device showed that the Caddie was leaving the housing development again. They began driving down a broad thoroughfare that led even farther from the center of the city. Bolan zoomed out even more on the map as they fell farther behind the car they were following.

"Where the hell are they going?" Paxton said out loud.

The Executioner frowned. "I don't know," he said. "But it looks like they may be leaving Amsterdam altogether." At the top of the screen, he could see a small icon that announced they were nearing the junction with Highway A4. He zoomed out even more and saw that they were at the southeast corner of the city.

Next to him, Paxton glanced his way. "How much range do we have before we lose the signal?" he asked.

"Five to ten miles," Bolan said. "Give or take a couple. It depends on the weather and other radio frequencies in the area that could interfere with the signal." He concentrated on the screen again. It was possible that Ali and the gold Cadillac were still driving in circles, trying to spot a tail. But the longer they drove, the more the Executioner's gut told him that wasn't the case. He would have bet every round in his Beretta and Desert Eagle that Ali and Hassan were indeed about to leave Amsterdam. That didn't worry him. Even if they took Highway A4 and joined what would be much lighter traffic outside of the city at night, he and Paxton could drop the BMW back far enough to stay well hidden.

A few minutes later, the Executioner's instincts proved correct when the blinking dot on the screen moved up an access ramp onto A4. "They're taking the highway south," he told Paxton.

"What highway?" the Ranger asked.

"The one you come to in another mile or so," the Executioner directed, and even as the words left his mouth they saw a sign announcing A4 coming up on the right-hand side of the road.

Paxton guided the BMW up the ramp and onto the main road. As Bolan had suspected, traffic was much lighter. But darkness had fallen completely by now, and all he could make out ahead of him were taillights. That was the downside.

The upside was that all Ali would be able to see in his rearview mirror were unidentifiable headlights.

The conversation coming from the transmitter had quieted. In its place came an eerie, haunting music in minor keys. Apparently Ali had loaded a cassette tape or CD. Occasionally, the ghostly voice of a singer chanted a few lines in Arabic.

"It's some kind of prayer song to Allah," Paxton said without being asked. "I can't make it all out. But I can tell you one thing."

"What's that?" Bolan asked.

"It'll never make the Billboard charts."

A moment later, they passed a green sign with white lettering that announced they were on their way toward Ring, and then the larger city of Haarlemmermeer. There was nothing to do but drive on. Once in a while, a few brief words would be passed between Ali and Hassan. Paxton was able to pick most of them up. But it was only meaningless small talk, and they learned nothing further until the Ranger suddenly said, "Abdul just asked him where, exactly, they were going."

Bolan started to speak but Paxton held up a hand, frowning down at the receiver. Ali's voice spoke a few more words, then the conversation died again. "Ali told Abdul he'd know where they were going when they got there," the Ranger translated. "His voice didn't sound particularly friendly."

The Executioner looked up from the screen, toward the lights on the highway ahead of him, knowing even before he looked that he would not be able to determine which set belonged to the Cadillac. At this point, things could still go well. But the situation had every possibility of turning nasty, too.

If Ali suspected Hassan of being a plant, the two men could be on their way to some remote Hands of Allah compound to find out exactly who Hassan was, what he knew and whom he was working for.

Before they killed him.

A second later, it became clear that Hassan might think that was a possibility himself. After a short few words that sounded like a question—which came in Ali's voice—Bolan heard Hassan say in English, "Just a little."

He turned toward the U.S. Army Ranger behind the wheel.

"Ali asked him if he spoke any English," Paxton said.

Bolan sat back in his seat. Hassan had answered in *English*. Which had been their prearranged code for the fact that he was in trouble.

But was that what his change in language really meant under these conditions? The Executioner had to take it in context. Wouldn't anyone who was asked if he spoke any language respond in that language if he could?

Maybe. Maybe not.

So what had the words "Just a little" actually meant? That Hassan didn't want Ali to know the true extent of his grasp of English, or that the informant had sensed that he was in grave danger?

The Executioner didn't know. And short of calling the man on his cell phone—which was out of the question with Ali in the Cadillac with him—he could see no possible way of finding out.

At least for the time being.

FOR WHAT WAS probably the tenth or twelfth time that night, Phil Paxton awakened, turned onto his other side and closed his eyes again. The chill from both the damp environment and the semishock in which his brain still swam hadn't dissipated, and he judged that he slept no more than forty-five minutes at a time before the cold or the discomfort or the fear in his heart forced his eyes open again. He had played football and baseball in high school, and now every injury he had ever received ached like that of an old man with arthritis. Which made him wonder why he had ever played such games in the first place.

But almost as soon as the question entered his mind, the answer followed.

That answer was *Brick*. His brother had been an All-State running back and star pitcher with the most wickedly breaking curve ball any high school had ever seen. So he, Phil, was expected to follow in his brother's footsteps. He wasn't expected to be as good as Brick, perhaps. But he was expected to at least try. So he had spent a lot of time at football practice holding blocking dummies, and most of every game on the sidelines. In baseball, the dugout had been his home except for when he warmed up the pitchers between innings while the real catcher got into his chest protector, shin guards and face mask.

In reality, he suspected that the only reason neither the football or baseball coach had cut him from the squads was because of their love and respect for Brick.

Brick, Brick, Brick. It seemed that was the only word he had ever heard until he'd finally graduated and left their small city for college.

Phil rolled over onto his other side again, trying out a new leg position by pulling his knees up toward his chest. It took a little of the stiffness out of his back—at least for a while—and his thoughts returned to his brother.

It was funny, he knew, that even though he had grown up in his brother's shadow, he had never resented Brick. One reason was that Brick had never acted as if he was better than Phil. Phil's older brother had spent so much time with him, and told him over and over and over that *he* didn't expect Phil to be anything but what he already was. Brick had encouraged his younger brother's interest in science, and when Phil's project took first prize in the state science fair his sophomore year, Brick had been there, on his feet and clapping louder than anyone, when Phil walked across the stage to accept the trophy.

It was a lot like what Phil did when Brick scored a touchdown or pitched a no-hitter.

The lighting in the wet cell hadn't changed since Phil had first awakened. So he had no way of knowing if it was really day or night. But out of habit, he raised his manacled hands and tried to see the luminous face on his Pulsar chronograph. What he saw was a bare wrist because his captors had taken the watch. The chronograph had been a gift from Brick last Christmas and, at the time, he had been a little sorry that it wasn't one of the big, sturdy chronographs that the Rangers and Green Berets and Navy SEALs wore. But now he was grateful.

Having his abductors take a chronograph off his wrist that was U.S. Special Forces issue didn't sound like a real good idea right now. As it was, if questioned, he could pass himself off as nothing more than a jogger—which he was—who liked the split-time feature.

Unable to return to sleep again, Phil guessed it had to be close to morning. The drug that had rendered him unconscious meant he couldn't be sure how long he'd been out. But his instincts told him it had not been for more than a couple of hours. When he had begun to get sleepy a few hours earlier, he'd just assumed it was close to his normal bedtime. He was a creature of habit, rising at the same time five days a week, and retiring at 11:00. On weekends, he and Janie slept a little later and stayed up watching old movies until 1:00 or 2:00 a.m., at most. Usually, by then, she had drifted off in his arms on the couch and he carried her into the bedroom.

The thought of his fiancée brought new pain to Phil's heart. Would he ever see her again? Would she ever know that he had, more or less, made his decision to marry her the first night he'd been in Amsterdam, and that he'd stayed true to her in spite of all the temptation around him?

Anxiety came over him now, and Phil sat up and scooted back against the cold, hard stones again. His shirt had never dried out, and he wondered what molds and funguses grew in whatever this age-old building was in which he was imprisoned. He was not a hypochondriac by any means. But he *was* a scientist, and he knew certain bacteria could thrive in such environments, enter the human body and make you sick or even kill you months later.

That was what had happened to the first explorers inside Egypt's great pyramids, people now knew. It had not been some Pharaoh's Curse, as the superstitious believed. Unless, of course, the pharaohs had put these natural diseases there themselves, he supposed.

The thought almost made Phil smile. He felt the muscles in his cheeks attempt the expression.

But they couldn't quite form it.

Instead, Phil glanced around the stone room. Five more people—all men—had been dragged into the room and bound with handcuffs and chains during the night. All of them were still asleep from whatever drug it was that had been administered to them.

But the man Phil had seen brought in first was beginning to come around. Phil could tell by the fact that he was starting to move and making small moaning sounds as he grew closer to consciousness. Which meant that, given a couple of hours or so either way, if the same drug, in the same amount, had been injected into both of them, Phil had been out longer than he had at first suspected. He might even have lost a full day.

The voices speaking Arabic could still be heard outside the tiny window in the door. Phil didn't know if the men guarding them cared if they talked or not. But he saw no reason to take chances. As the man next to him came around, he ground an elbow lightly into his ribs. "Hey," he whispered.

The man lying next to him opened his eyes, then shut them again. He had dark blond-brown hair that grew down over both ears. It was hard to tell in the dim light, but he also appeared to have grown one of those extremely short mustaches and goatees popular with so many young men these days. Phil had always wondered if they actually liked them that wispy, or if that was as thick as they could grow them at their age.

"Hey," he whispered again.

The man opened his eyes this time and looked around. Phil reached over as best he could in his handcuffs and chains and helped him up to a sitting position against the wall.

The blond man shivered just as Phil had done when the cold wet wall met his spine.

"Do you have any idea where we are?" Phil whispered.

The man shook his head. "I *was* in Zaanstad," he said, naming a Dutch city northeast of Amsterdam. "Are we still there?"

"I don't know but I doubt it," Phil said quietly. The man's accent was as Midwestern U.S. as you could get and, for some reason, Phil took great comfort in that fact. "I was in Amsterdam." He paused a moment, then asked, "What's your name, where are you from and how did they get you?"

"Name's George Johns," came the response. "From Kansas City. On the Kansas side, not Missouri." But before he could answer the third question, his face covered over in confusion. He looked at the ceiling, squinting, as if trying to remember. "I was traveling with Nan. That's my girlfriend. She went into this shop and…" His voice trailed off. Several seconds passed, then he said, "The next thing I remember is…you."

"You saw your girlfriend go in the shop?" Phil asked.

George Johns thought hard again. "Yes. I remember a little bell ringing when the door closed behind her. It was tied to the doorknob."

Phil took a deep breath. There were still four other people bound and unconscious from the drugs on the other side of the stone cell. As best Phil could tell, they were all men. But there was not enough light coming through the window to make out distinct features, and he recognized none of them. But, then, there was no reason he should. George Johns, on the other hand, would more than likely know if his girlfriend, Nan, was one of them. Women didn't dress that much differently than men when backpacking through Europe these days. And what he was about to do would be a good test as to just how lucid George Johns had become.

Phil hated to ask. But he had to. "Have your eyes adjusted to this lighting?" he said.

"About as well as they're going to, I think," Johns said.

"Then take a look across the room. There are four

women over there, still unconscious. None of them were brought in at the same time you were—keep that in mind. But you'd better look hard and see if Nan might be one of them anyway."

A new jolt of fear came over Johns's face as the possibility that his girlfriend might have been kidnapped, too, dawned on him. He leaned forward, his eyelids rising almost comically high as he studied the sleeping figures. Gradually, his face grew puzzled rather than frightened. "Those are *men,* not women," he said, letting out his breath for the first time since he'd started looking.

Phil breathed a sigh of relief himself. Johns's mind was functioning at least reasonably well. Now, he knew, if a chance to escape presented itself, he just might have an ally who could help him.

At this point, the other captives were still more drugged-out zombies who'd be more liabilities than assets.

But there was another reason he had asked George Johns the question in the manner he had. Phil wanted Johns to begin realizing that things *could* be worse. A positive attitude was always more successful than a negative one. Granted, being here, where they were, was bad enough. But to have the woman you loved—like Phil loved Janie and Johns probably did Nan—in such a position with you would be all but unbearable.

"Just checking to see how alert you were," Phil said, forcing a little chuckle he didn't really feel from his chest. "You say you watched Nan go into the shop?"

"Yes. I distinctly remember that. But nothing after."

"Then that means they came at you from behind," Phil said. "Grabbed you and had the needle in your arm before you even knew they were there. They must have had a car waiting a few feet away on the street."

George Johns shrugged. "I guess," he said. "But *why?*

Nan and I are both just college students. Wichita State. We don't have any money for ransom. And our parents aren't rich, either."

"Ransom isn't the reason we were taken," Phil said. "It's politics."

"Terrorists?" Johns said, his mouth falling open.

"Didn't you see the way these guys are dressed?" Phil asked. Then he answered his own question. "No, I guess you wouldn't have since they grabbed you from the back and you were out until just now. I hate to tell you, but we're in the hands of some kind of radical Muslim organization."

"Oh, shit," Johns said. He closed his eyes for a moment, then opened them again, and Phil wondered if he'd used the time for a brief prayer of deliverance. "Then they're going to kill us no matter what?" Johns finally asked, although it came out sounding more like a statement than a question.

"Unless we get rescued or escape," Phil said. "But yes, that's their plan. As soon as they've gotten all of the publicity they can squeeze out of us, my guess is that we're all as good as dead."

"When will that be?" Johns's voice quavered slightly as he spoke now.

"Who knows?" Phil said. "Today? Tomorrow? Three years from now? There's no way to tell." He thought for a moment, then decided it would do the young college student no good to dwell on such a grisly subject. So he changed it. "You said you were a college student at Wichita State. What are you majoring in?"

"Business administration," George Johns said. "What do you do?"

Phil wasn't about to admit to *anyone* that he was a nuclear research scientist. In fact, if he ever got out of here he might even tell Janie he'd changed careers and forgotten all he ever knew about the subject. Maybe that wouldn't even be a lie.

Right now, he'd have rather been a garbage collector who lived in a trailer park than who he actually was.

But Phil was what he was, and he knew he'd need a cover story. Something he could stick to with everyone—hostage and terrorist alike—and something he could back up if necessary. His mind flew back to the summer after Brick's senior year in high school when he and his brother had both worked for a construction company during the day and partied at night. A lot of times, Brick even took him along with the celebrating seniors who were enjoying their last few weeks together before heading off to lead separate lives at separate colleges or jobs.

It had made Phil feel like a king. Well, maybe not like a king. But like the king's brother, and that wasn't such a bad feeling, either.

"I'm in the construction business," Phil said. The words were barely out of his mouth when the sound of the key being inserted into the old wooden door echoed off the stone walls of the room. The two men stopped talking, and their eyes shot toward the noise in time to see a tall man with a full beard enter the room. He wore a traditional robe and headdress, but extending down past the hem of the robe were the legs of a pair of desert camouflage pants and sand-colored combat boots.

Phil had seen him before. He had helped drag in one of the men during the night, and all of the other kidnappers had obviously deferred to him as their leader.

The room was brighter now with the door open, and the man took three steps inside the cell before stopping to scan both sides of the small room. He looked first to Phil Paxton and George Johns, then to the men still sleeping. "You are the only two awake?" he asked in heavily accented English.

Phil felt a sudden anger come over him. He was not a fighter like his brother, Brick—never had been. But suddenly, he *felt* like one. "Nothing much passes by you unnoticed, does it?" he said sarcastically.

The man's accent might have been strong, but his command of the English language was good enough to catch the nuance. He smiled in what almost looked like sadness, then walked over to where Phil was seated and kicked him in the abdomen.

Phil grunted and bent forward, his head almost going down to his knees. The wind had left his lungs and now he struggled to inhale but couldn't catch his breath. Looking up, he saw the bearded man sneer.

Then the terrorist looked toward George Johns. "You two are the only ones awake?" he asked again.

Johns wasn't about to make the same mistake Phil had. "Yes, sir," he replied immediately.

"Then I will interview the two of you first," said the bearded man. "And I will start with *you,* since your friend appears to need time to catch his breath again." He let out a high, shrieking laugh that was worse than fingernails screeching down a chalkboard, and Phil couldn't help wondering if the laugh came naturally or had been developed and practiced with the sole purpose of tormenting anyone forced to hear it.

"You may call me Dawud A.," the terrorist said as he reached down, grabbed George Johns by the collar of his shirt and hauled him to his feet. He produced a key and began unlocking the man's restraints. "We are going to have a little private talk, you and I." Holding Johns by the arm, he guided him toward the door.

Just before he left the dank stone cell, Dawud looked back over his shoulder.

The air was just now returning to Phil lungs. He sat up straight, wishing for all he was worth that he had Dawud's beard in one hand and the custom-made, cactus-handled knife he'd given Brick for his birthday the previous year, in the other.

"I will be back for you when I am finished with this one," Dawud said. "So, until then, I would ask you to welcome everyone for me as they awaken. Tell them if you would please, that they are safe in the Hands of Allah." Without waiting for a response, he laughed again, turned and left the room.

Phil heard the key slide the bolt locked again and sat back against the cold wet stone. He looked up at the ceiling, still panting from the kick. Two things, however, bothered him even more than Dawud's boot had.

He still couldn't remember if he'd brought his government ID along or not but he suspected it was still on his dresser at home. If Dawud had found it in his passport case, he would have been the *first* subject to be interviewed, out of breath or not.

But what worried Phil Paxton the most was what Dawud had said just before leaving. *They were safe in the Hands of Allah.*

Was it just an expression, or should the statement be taken literally? Phil didn't know. He hoped it had simply been a figure of speech. But in the back of his mind, he feared it might not be. While his knowledge of the Islamic terrorism in the Netherlands was severely limited, he knew at least one thing: the Hands of Allah was the worst of the many cells working out of Amsterdam. They had been responsible for more bombings, random shootings, assassinations of government officials and kidnappings than any other criminal or terrorist group in Europe.

And they had *never* had a hostage rescued.

Or left any American alive when they were finished with him.

7

Dawud A. sat back in the rickety wooden chair, away from the table in the room next to what he had dubbed his "examination area."

It sounded so much better—far more professional—than "torture chamber."

Crossing his legs, the leader of the Hands of Allah reached forward and lifted a tiny cup of strong thick Arabic coffee he so loved, and took a sip. He remembered his days in the United States when he had attended the University of Nebraska and the weak, watery coffee they had served at all of the backwoods cafés and truck stops. It had been so thin you could see all the way through the liquid to the white ceramic bottom of the cup. It seemed they used those same white cups in every such café in Nebraska. And even in the other states he had visited. He had hated the cups, hated the coffee. It had not been coffee at all. More like coffee-flavored water, and it served as a metaphor for his feelings about the U.S. itself.

America was watered-down. Phony. More concerned with appearance than depth—more interested in the body than the soul.

Dawud hated America even more than its coffee, and while he knew that the years he had spent in Nebraska were necessary training in order to understand his enemy, they had hardly been pleasant.

The Arabic coffee he now sipped symbolized his return to the life to which he had been fated by Allah to return. But it, too, had now grown lukewarm as if becoming another metaphor for the mistake he knew he had just made. So he downed it in one gulp, then poured another cup from the carafe on the hot plate attached to the small generator in the basement of the old castle.

Dawud looked up at the wooden beams overhead, wondering just how old the castle might be. He guessed it had first been constructed during the Middle Ages, during the period when the Christian infidels of Europe had been hell-bent on retaking the Holy Land with their Crusades. The building, sitting behind its high wall almost in the exact center of the city, had been abandoned for the past fifty years. Its ownership had passed through several hands during that half-century. Each new owner had planned to renovate the castle and turn it into a tourist attraction of some sort, which would have been typical of the decedent Western business world. No one had followed through with their plans, however, and Dawud—using the front company Middle Eastern Investments—had purchased the run-down castle for a song.

Dawud remembered the look on the broker's face when he told the man he eventually planned to turn the castle into the largest mosque in the Netherlands. The man had not wanted to argue—in fact, he would have preferred not to even have had such information. True Muslims, such as himself, men who knew that the only way to serve Allah was by force, had infiltrated the Netherlands to such an extent that native Hollanders, and even the government, stood in both awe and fear of them. The face of the man brokering the deal had told him that he feared if the castle sale fell through, his entire family might be murdered.

Dawud laughed softly to himself. That broker might have been right.

Taking another sip of coffee, Dawud sat back in his chair. The castle was perfect for his purposes—centrally located yet easy to slip in and out of unnoticed. True, it was cold and damp, especially in the basement where this room, the examination area and the dungeon were located. But that was fine with him. He and his men had only to stay in this area of the castle for short lengths of time, and all of the men imprisoned in the dungeon were Americans. It was about time that such rich, spoiled heathens learned a little about the discomfort with which the rest of the world had to live on a daily basis.

Dawud finished his coffee and poured another small cup. The castle's location had other advantages, as well. His men could snatch their hostages right off the streets of Amsterdam or in nearby towns and have them shackled in the dungeon long before the morphine injected into their arms wore off. This kept the captives in a constant state of confusion. They didn't know how long they'd been unconscious when they woke up, and therefore had no idea about where they were.

That was just one of a number of things that kept them off balance, and men who were off balance were far more likely to talk and cooperate than those who weren't.

Dawud set the coffee cup back in its tiny saucer. Next to the saucer, on the splintery wooden table that had probably been in the room since the castle was built, was an open copy of the Koran. He reached out and closed the book, moving it away from the cup, saucer and hot plate to keep from soiling it.

As Dawud continued to sit and think, pondering the mistake he had allowed to happen and how to correct it, he looked through the open doorway to the examination area. Two of his top men, Jabbar and Khalid, were unstrapping the leather restraints from the wrists and ankles of the man he now suspected was actually named George Johns. When the buckles had been unfastened, they lifted the lifeless form by the arms and legs and began carrying him toward the staircase that led upward to the castle's ground floor.

With each step they took, droplets of blood dripped from the dead man's body onto the stone floor. Dawud wondered for a moment if he should order the mess cleaned up, then decided against it. Seeing the blood would have a profound effect on the next man he "examined." It would be one more way of unbalancing that man's brain.

But the sight of the corpse being hauled away angered Dawud. Not because he had killed the wrong man but because this man named Johns—if that was actually his name—had been a tough nut to crack. And that had meant a loss of valuable *time*.

A few minutes later, Dawud heard Jabbar and Khalid coming back down the ancient stone steps. The American's body, he knew, would have been thrown into the floor-to ceiling fireplace located in the great room just above them. Other Hands of Allah men tended the fire around the clock, and eventually there would be nothing left of George Johns except, perhaps, his teeth and a few bone fragments.

Jabbar and Khalid entered the room where Dawud sat and stood silently on the other side of the table. Jabbar met Dawud A.'s eyes. But Khalid looked down at the floor, then up, then around, uneasily.

"I am sorry for the mistake," Jabbar said, and his voice reflected sincerity. "Somehow the passports got mixed up and out of order."

Dawud shook his head. "I do not blame you, Jabbar, for this mistake." Then, turning to Khalid, he said, "But Khalid, did I not give you *distinct* instructions that the passports should be numbered, and that a corresponding number be written with a permanent marker on the wrist of the man to which each document belonged?"

Finally Khalid looked at him. And Dawud saw the broken veins that made the white around the man's eyes look pink. "You did," Khalid said. "I have no excuse except that in the excitement of it all, I forgot."

"You are correct." Dawud nodded. "That is no excuse. Tell me, Khalid, why do you think we chose to kidnap seven Americans instead of only the one we wanted?"

"As cover, of course," Khalid replied. "To make it appear that the kidnappings were at random."

"And why do you believe I had our Islamic comrades from Berlin come to Amsterdam to perform the actual kidnappings instead of just using men like you or Jabbar?"

"You did not tell us," Khalid said, and now his eyes were wandering around the room again. He scratched his left wrist for a second with his right hand, then suddenly stopped as if it might have been some unforgivable sin. "But it was my opinion that if there were witnesses, the men actually grabbing the Americans would be long gone—back in Germany—before they could be identified."

"So far," Dawud said, "you are correct. Which is why, of course, I cannot just call those men in and ask which of the prisoners is the man we wanted."

Khalid's eyes fell to the floor once more. His right hand started toward his left wrist again, then stopped and returned to his side. "I can only say I am sorry," he mumbled under his breath.

"Khalid, Khalid, Khalid," Dawud said, shaking his head in disgust and standing up from his chair. "Come around the table, please."

Khalid looked up again, his eyes suddenly filled not with fear but horror. "Why?" he asked.

"Come around the table, Khalid," Dawud said in the same calm voice.

Slowly, apprehensively, Khalid took a step to the side of the table where Dawud already stood.

As soon as he did, Dawud reached out with both hands and grabbed the man's left arm. Rolling up the sleeve of his *abaya,* he saw the track marks—some already beginning to form ulcers—on the inside of Khalid's elbow.

"So," said Dawud. "It appears you have taken your own liking to the morphine we use during our abductions."

"Please!" Khalid said, suddenly frantic. "Hear me out before you condemn me!"

"I am listening," Dawud replied. He continued to hold Khalid's arm with both hands.

"It was an accident," Khalid said in a trembling voice.

"Ah, I see," Dawud spoke softly yet sarcastically. "You *accidentally* filled a syringe with the morphine meant to knock out one of the men we have kidnapped, then *accidentally* stuck the needle into your arm. Then, purely by accident, your thumb pushed the plunger down and injected the drug into your arm. And by the looks of your arm, this *accident* happened over, and over, and over." He paused, drew in a breath or air, then said, "Khalid, my dear friend, you must indeed be the clumsiest man Allah has ever created."

"No," Khalid said, and now his voice came in a frantic whisper. "The *first time* really was an accident." He took several deep breaths before going on. "It was when we captured the American oilman. The one from Texas. Last year—you remember?"

"Of course I remember," Dawud almost spit. "His money

has financed most of this operation. And his fat body was eaten by swine."

"Yes, yes, that is the one!" Khalid almost shouted now. "When we took him out of the cab, he fought us. I aimed the needle for his arm, it moved, and I accidentally stuck it into my own thigh."

Dawud turned to Jabbar. The two men had been together on that abduction. It had not been important enough to recruit out-of-town Muslims.

Jabbar nodded. "I remember it," he said. "I had a second syringe. I had to stick it into the man's thick neck."

"Yes!" Khalid shouted. "Yes, that is true!"

"But that does not explain the multitude of injections I see here," Dawud said.

"No, it does not," Khalid agreed. "But when the morphine entered my system, something happened. Something I would not have dreamed possible while still on this Earth."

"And what was that?" Dawud asked, although he knew what the answer would be.

"I caught a glimpse of…Paradise," Khalid said, his eyes looking as dreamy now in remembrance of that first morphine high as if it had just happened. "I suddenly felt at peace with Allah and all mankind." He coughed nervously, then said, "Certainly, Dawud, you can understand why I wanted to repeat the experience."

Dawud did his best to hide his disgust. "Of course I can understand it," he said. "When I was at the University of Nebraska, living in a student dormitory, many young men took a drug called LSD. Some told me later that they had seen God."

"Yes, yes!" Khalid said. "They undoubtedly did!"

"How could they?" Dawud asked. "They were *Christians,* if they had any religion at all, and I suspect they did not. So can you explain to me why Allah would reveal himself to an infidel?"

The expression on Khalid's face fell as the short period of hope suddenly evaporated. At first, he remained silent. Then, after a few seconds, he played his final card. "Perhaps Allah was trying to speak to them? To convert them to the true religion? And they denied him?"

Jabbar knew what was coming and he had taken a step back. Now Dawud looked to him. "Jabbar, did *you* know about this?" he asked, shaking Khalid's arm up and down with both hands.

Jabbar shook his head. "I suspected something was wrong several times," he said. "But I did not know it was drugs."

Dawud nodded his belief in the man's statement, then turned his eyes back to Khalid. "You are not an infidel, Khalid," he said as he dropped the man's arm with his right hand, continuing to hold on to it with his left. "You are worse than an infidel. You have been shown the truth, yet you desert that truth for one of the false gods of the Americans. *Drugs*."

When Khalid looked down in shame, Dawud shouted, "Look up! Look up at me! Look at me in the eyes!"

At the same time Khalid did so, Dawud jerked the same *khanjar* with which he had cut George Johns's throat from the sheath on his belt. With a lightning-fast backhand slash, he drew the curved blade across Khalid's neck, severing the jugular, muscles, tendons, ligaments, and feeling the edge even slash across the front of the man's spine.

Almost headless, Khalid fell to the floor.

"Pick another man from upstairs and carry him to the same fire we use for all of the infidels," Dawud ordered Jabbar.

Expressionless, as if he watched men beheaded every day, Jabbar nodded. "I think it will be nothing compared to the fire in which he will burn from now unto eternity," he said. Then he turned and hurried out of the room, returning a few minutes later with another man. Together, they carted Khalid's body out of sight.

Dawud looked at the massive amount of blood on the floor. The droplets that had fallen from George Johns's body as he was carried off were not even comparable to the river that now ran past the front of the old table. He wondered for a moment if he should bring the next candidate in for examination while the blood was still fresh.

No, Dawud thought as he sat back down and sipped again at his coffee. It had grown cold once more, so he freshened the cup from the carafe on the hot plate. There was a better, faster way to handle this foul-up.

Reaching into a pocket inside his *abaya*, Dawud pulled out a cell phone and tapped in a number he had memorized in his heart. A moment later, a man's voice answered. "I told you *never* to call me on this line!" the voice said in Arabic, using what could only be described as a shouting whisper. "As it so happens, I am alone at the moment. But you had no way of knowing that!"

"Then it is to both of our best interests that we keep this conversation as short as possible," Dawud said sarcastically. He didn't like the man he had just called, and he didn't like working with him. But it was necessary. "I need you to come to the castle."

"What!" the voice said in the same whisper-shout. "Are you out of your mind? I can't just pick up and leave! What am I supposed to tell—"

Again, Dawud interrupted the man. "What you use as your excuse to leave is not my concern. But surely a man as creative as yourself can think of something plausible."

"Why do you need me?" the voice demanded.

"There has been a mixup with the passports," Dawud said. "We are unable to tell which man is Phillip Paxton."

"Well, look at the *pictures* in the passports," the voice said.

"Do you think me too stupid to not have already done that?" Dawud replied. He made a mental note to order the death of the man on the other end of the line just as soon as he was no longer needed. "They look too much alike. And I do not want to waste time interrogating all of them in order to find out which one is the nuclear scientist."

There was a long sigh on the other end of the line. "All right," the voice finally said. "But this is going to be dangerous. I'll expect something more out of it than I'm already getting."

Dawud smiled as he remembered his decision a few moments earlier to kill the man. "Name your own price," he said.

"We'll talk about it when I get there. Now, I want to get off the line while I'm still alone."

"Then goodbye," said Dawud. "I will see you as soon as you get here."

"It might be a while. I have to come up with some excuse—"

"Come up with it *fast*." Dawud allowed a certain level of threat to enter his tone of voice.

"I'll be there as soon as I can."

Both men hung up at the same time.

Jabbar and the new man—Harun—returned to the room as Dawud replaced the cell phone inside his robe.

"Would you like us to bring in another of the Americans?" Jabbar asked.

Dawud shook his head. "Go wash, change your clothes and say your prayers," he said. "I have my contact on his way to identify the real Phillip Paxton."

The two men nodded, bowed slightly, then turned and left.

Dawud allowed a smile to creep over his face. Soon he would have solved the problem of Phillip Paxton's identity.

And then he would take advantage of the fact that he had one of America's top nuclear scientists to do his bidding. He did not have access to all of the elements it would take to build a true nuclear bomb. But getting his hands on enough radioactive material to allow Phillip Paxton to construct what the American infidels liked to call "dirty bombs" would not be a problem. Soon, he would be able to kill thousands, if not hundreds of thousands, and make much of Amsterdam uninhabitable for many years to come.

That, in turn, would severely affect the diamond and other gem markets. Dawud laughed out loud. The rich daughters of Americans just might have to go without Dutch-cut diamond engagement rings for a while.

WITH NO OTHER OPTION AVAILABLE, Bolan and Paxton continued to use the homing device and laptop to follow the gold Cadillac. By now the Executioner had zoomed the map out to include a much wider area around Amsterdam.

He didn't have the slightest idea where this Koran study group was meeting, but he knew if he lost track of Hassan, at the very least, he'd lose valuable intelligence.

At worst, his informant would be murdered.

"This ain't lookin' so good," Brick Paxton said from behind the wheel of the BMW. "Eventually, they're going to turn off the highway. Then we're going to have to do the same. If the place they're headed is remote enough—and flat enough—they're going to spot us."

Bolan nodded. "No disagreement here," he said.

"So what do I do?" Paxton wanted to know.

"Exactly what you're doing now. Keep following them. We'll worry about being spotted—and find a way around it—when, and if, the time comes."

Bolan continued to watch the laptop. Suddenly, he

frowned. "They're slowing down," he said. "Looks like they're going to take the exit toward Aalsmeer."

"Aalsmeer?" Paxton said. "Never even heard of it."

"Neither have I," the Executioner told him. "But it's a little village several miles back southwest, according to this map." He stopped speaking for a moment as the Cadillac slowed even more. "Yeah, that's where they're headed, all right."

Paxton didn't have to be told to speed up. His foot pressed down harder on the accelerator. "Any intersecting roads between this highway and the village?" he asked.

"Uh-huh," the Executioner replied. "A couple. But that's not what worries me."

"What does?"

"The fact that there are probably *dozens* of rural roads that aren't marked on this map. We're getting into the heart of Holland's other flower-growing region. If they turn off on an unmarked route, we won't see it on the screen. It'll just look like they're driving across open country."

In his peripheral vision, Bolan saw Paxton frown. "Which means we're going to have to get close enough for a visual," he said, speaking the Executioner's thoughts for him. "And take the chance of being spotted."

"Exactly," Bolan said. Ahead, a green sign announcing the exit to toward Aalsmeer appeared in the headlights. "But for now, we may be okay. There should still be some other traffic—even if it's lighter—on this road."

Paxton slowed the BMW and took the exit. "Can you tell how far ahead of us they are?" he asked.

"Couple of miles, it looks like here. Speed up again. I want to be within a mile or so of them in case they turn off again. If the unmarked roads are too close together, we aren't going to be able to determine which one they took unless we actually see them."

Paxton made a right after stopping at the stop sign at the end of the off ramp, then floored the accelerator to pick up speed again. As the Executioner had guessed, there were a few other vehicles on the road. But the traffic was thin—too thin to risk getting any closer.

Bolan frowned as they passed a gravel road that didn't appear on the screen in front of him. He greatly doubted that the Cadillac's destination would be just off this two-lane blacktop road they were now speeding down. It was far more likely that the Koran study group met at a more remote location. So sooner or later, getting close enough to follow them by sight was going to be mandatory. He had some equipment in the bags that would help. But they would still have to risk being spotted.

Looking out the window, the Executioner saw that the moon was at almost three-quarters. The only thing worse for them was if it had been full.

They passed two more unmarked side roads, but the beeping dot on the laptop screen continued straight down the blacktop.

"You'd better close in on them," the Executioner said. "If we don't, we're going to lose them. These side roads are getting too close together to rely on guesswork."

"Okay," Paxton said, shrugging and leaning forward to coax even more speed out of the BMW. "But keep in mind that if we can see them, they can see us."

"Not necessarily," the Executioner said as he twisted toward the backseat. Unzipping the bag Paxton had carried out of the hotel, he rummaged through the gear inside until he found the two pairs of infrared night goggles he'd packed along. Then, turning back to the front, he dropped one pair into Paxton's lap. "As soon as you see them," he said, "put these on and kill the lights."

Paxton nodded his understanding.

A few seconds later, a dim pair of taillights appeared far ahead of them down the road.

"There they are," Paxton said. He pulled the goggles over his eyes and reached forward, shutting off the BMW's lights. Then he accelerated again, closing the gap between them and the Caddie even further. But almost as soon as he'd shut off the headlights, the taillights ahead disappeared again.

"We're going to have to risk getting even closer," the Executioner said, staring at the laptop screen. He still had his own night-vision resting on his knees as he monitored the screen. "They're going to be in and out of sight every time one of us climbs or descends a hill."

As Paxton sped up to close the gap even further, the voices coming in over the receiver suddenly caught Bolan's attention.

"So," the Executioner heard Hassan say in English. "How much farther is it?"

This time, there could be no other explanation as to why the informant had spoken in English.

He sensed trouble.

But the reply, whatever it was, from Ali came in Arabic.

"Did you pick that up?" the Executioner asked Paxton.

"Something along the lines of 'not too much farther' as best I could tell."

The dot on the screen suddenly slowed again, which meant the Cadillac was about to turn.

"Can you see them?" Bolan asked.

"Uh-uh," Paxton said. "They just disappeared on the other side of a hill."

"Floor it," Bolan ordered. "They're getting ready to turn off."

This time, Paxton seemed to put his whole body into the effort, pressing his right leg down until the BMW's speedometer registered over 100. Bolan watched as the dot on the screen continued to beep, but turned off the highway and began traveling across what looked like open country on the map.

"So," Hassan said over the airwaves, again in English. "Why are we turning here?"

"Because this is the route to the study group," Ali answered, switching languages himself this time, as well.

The Executioner closed the laptop and pulled his goggles over his face. The eerie, shadowy world of infrared allowed him to see clearly down the road. But the Cadillac was still out of sight. "Keep pushing it," he told Paxton. He watched the speedometer rise to 110. As they crested a hilltop, the village of Aalsmeer appeared a mile or so in the distance.

But no taillights between them and the village were visible.

The Cadillac had turned.

Paxton could see the same thing. "Any suggestions?" he asked.

Bolan stared ahead, trying to look out over the countryside to both their left and right, hoping to catch a glimpse of red taillights. But he couldn't.

Another gravel-road intersection appeared ahead and the Executioner said, "Slow down, but don't stop unless I tell you to." He continued to strain his eyes through the goggles, hoping against the odds that he might spot which way the Cadillac had turned.

As they neared the village of Aaslmeer, the gravel crossroads got even closer together than before. Paxton slowed the BMW at each one, but Bolan ordered him on.

Finally, when they were only a half mile or so from the village, they passed an intersection where the Executioner could see the final motes of dust—created by a vehicle turning off the blacktop—trying to settle back onto the ground. Even though Paxton had slowed as before, they were past the turnoff before Bolan could say, "There! They turned to the right!"

Paxton put as much weight into the brake as he had the accelerator, and the BMW's tires squealed in protest as the vehicle skidded into a fast U-turn. The Army Ranger laid more rubber on the blacktop as he took off again, doubling back the way they'd come, then passing through the settling dust as the vehicle turned onto the side road.

"We can thank God these roads aren't paved," Paxton said as he picked up speed again. "Without that dust, we'd have lost them."

Bolan nodded as he took off his goggles and opened the laptop again. Now that they knew they were on the right road, they could monitor Ali and Hassan on the laptop once more. But there would be absolutely *no other traffic* with which to blend into now, so Paxton kept the BMW dark and left his goggles on.

"I am sorry to sound like a child," came Hassan's voice over the receiver. "But I am anxious to meet the other members of the group. May I assume now that we are almost there?"

"Another half mile or so," Ali's voice said. "But tell me, why have you begun to speak in English?"

"Well," said Hassan, "you asked me if I spoke the language earlier. So I am practicing. I am not a genius, but neither am I a stupid man. I must assume that wherever we are going, and whatever we will be planning to do, will involve speaking English. So I will tell you more now—I am quite fluent in the language."

"And why have you studied it so?" asked Ali.

"Because," Hassan said in a very convincing voice, "the more you know about your enemy, the easier it is to kill him." There was a short pause, then the informant went on. "I think it is about time we stop playing these games, Ali. I know we are not planning to sit around on the carpet and study the Koran tonight."

"You are correct," Ali's voice came back, and Bolan was glad that Hassan had come up with the idea of using English as the distress signal. It also allowed him to more fully understand exactly what was going on.

"But if you were serious about the things you told me earlier," Ali went on, "I think you will be pleased with what we have planned. And I think you will want to be a part of it."

The dot on the screen made a slight turn to the left, then stopped beeping, which meant that the Cadillac had stopped.

Wherever it was they were going, Ali and Hassan were there.

"Slow her down," Bolan ordered Paxton. "They've stopped. Somewhere just off this road."

The Ranger reduced the BMW's speed to a crawl.

"Ah, we are here," Hassan said over the airwaves. "But one thing bothers me."

"What is that?" asked Ali.

"You said that if I was *serious* about what I had said earlier I would be happy to be part of this. Why would you question my seriousness?"

"Because," Ali said, and his words were accompanied by the unmistakable sound of the slide on an automatic pistol being pulled back to chamber a round, "you might very well be a plant. A spy of some kind."

Paxton stopped the BMW altogether as he and the Executioner continued to listen.

"And to tell you the truth," Ali continued, "that is *exactly* what I think you are."

"Please," Hassan said, his voice trembling slightly. "That is not the case. And there is no reason to hold that gun against my head. I am *one of you*."

"We will see," Ali said, and from the receiver came the sounds of the Cadillac's doors opening and shutting again. "When we get inside, and you meet the other men."

"But how?" Hassan asked as Bolan and Paxton listened to the faint sounds of the men's footsteps. "If you suspect me, why did you bring me in the first place?"

"Because if you are the spy I believe you to be, we will want to know all that you know about us." A hideous laugh followed the statement, and then the man holding the gun on their informant ended with, "And believe me, we have a thousand ways to encourage you to share with us all of the information you have."

The sounds of feet moving up wooden steps were audible as the men's voices stopped. A moment later, a door opened and closed.

Then Ali said something in Arabic that Bolan couldn't understand.

But Paxton caught it. "This is the man I told you about," the Army Ranger repeated in English. "Who would like to be the first to force him to tell us all about himself?"

8

Brick Paxton started to throw the BMW back into Drive, but the Executioner reached out and grabbed his arm. "Wait," he ordered.

"Wait?" Paxton almost shouted. "What do you mean, wait? They're gonna kill him!"

"No, they aren't," Bolan said, shaking his head. "At least not for a while. They want to find out which side he's really on first. And if he's against them, they'll want to know what he knows about *them* first."

"So, you want to just sit here and let them torture his ass for a while?" Paxton asked incredulously.

The Executioner could understand the man's confusion. Paxton had proved to be an excellent warrior, and he deserved an explanation concerning Bolan's hesitancy. "That won't happen for a while, either. If it does at all," he said.

"Shouldn't we at least make a quick drive-by and check on the layout?" the Army Ranger asked.

"That'd be like cutting Abdul's throat ourselves at this point," the Executioner answered. Before Paxton could question him further, he said, "Since we turned onto this road, have you seen any other traffic besides the Caddie and us?"

"No," Paxton said.

"Then if you were one of the men in the house, and you

suddenly saw another car coming down the road right after Ali and Abdul got there, wouldn't you at least suspect there was some connection?"

Paxton had kept his hand on the gearshift. But now he dropped his arm back into his lap, sat back against his seat and blew air through his lips. "Yeah," he said. "Even with the lights off they'd hear us coming and could probably see the car through the windows in this moon."

"We'd look even *more* suspicious with the lights off," Bolan said.

"But what are we supposed to do, then?"

"Wait," Bolan said. "We already have our blacksuits on under these *abaya,* and our weapons and other gear are ready to go at a second's notice. Let's just give it a little time. Get the feel of things. Then we'll go."

"Okay," Paxton said.

The two men waited patiently, listening to the receiver. On occasion, Paxton picked up a few words and phrases and translated them into English, but it all sounded like small talk.

Suddenly Hassan switched to English again. "Ali asked if I could speak English," he said, sounding indignant. "I can. Is *that* the reason you suspect me of being a traitor to Allah? If so, then Ali must be a traitor, as well, because he speaks English, too. And so must be everyone else in this house who understands my words now, miles and miles away from any other people or buildings except that deserted barn we saw on our way in. Is this isolation so no one will hear the screams of the innocent who you torture?" Before any of the Hands of Allah men could reply, he added, "There are *many* reasons to speak English in this war of ours. Many, *many* reasons to do so, even right now."

"That was for us," the Executioner said. "He's telling us that things are about to get hairy. And that there's only the one house in the area, and not to waste time searching the barn." He took a deep breath and his right hand moved unconsciously toward the grip of the Calico 950 hanging on the strap under his arm. "Let's move. But drive slow. As soon as we see the house, we'll ditch the car and hoof it on in."

Paxton did as commanded, keeping their speed down to twenty miles per hour as the arguing returned to Arabic. With their lights still off, both men now wore their infrared night-vision goggles. Paxton guided the BMW up and down several hills. The strain on the man's face told the Executioner it was taking all of the Ranger's willpower to keep from flooring the accelerator.

Finally, the BMW crested a hill and they saw the house just to the left of the road. It was roughly a quarter of a mile away, and the shadowy shapes of the barn Hassan had mentioned, as well as a traditional Dutch windmill, could be made out in the moonlight behind what was either a two-story or split-level structure.

"Okay," the Executioner said, "that has to be it." He turned and looked out the rear window. "Throw us in Reverse and back the car back down the hill, out of sight of the house."

Paxton did as instructed, and thirty seconds later the BMW was parked, the engine off, on the side of the lonely dirt road. Bolan looked down at the radio receiver. He had an earplug that would enable him to continue listening to what was going on inside the house without the sound giving them away. But the receiver itself was bulky, and the men were speaking rapidly in Arabic again and he couldn't understand a word. Giving the receiver and earplug to Paxton wouldn't be much better. The Ranger's limited grasp of the language, especially when it was spoken as fast as the men inside the house were speaking, didn't offset the problems taking the receiver would present.

In any case the voices inside the house were growing more

angry, and it appeared that Abdul Hassan was losing ground in the argument.

It was time to act.

Since both men were exiting the vehicle at the same time, Bolan drew the Beretta and used the grip to break out the interior light. Part of him told himself that it was nothing short of a miracle that none of the Hands of Allah men had yet thought to rip open Hassan's robe and check for bugs.

But another part of him was beginning to think it might not be so strange after all. The bottom line was that Hassan hadn't really done much to help them so far. And there was always the chance that he was playing both sides. But even if he was on the level, sooner or later the men inside the house would find both the transmitter and Nagra. Then there would be no question as to whether Hassan was a plant.

Unless that other part of the Executioner's brain—the part that had begun nagging at him for the simple reason that too much time had already elapsed since Hassan entered the house with nothing bad happening to him—turned out to be correct.

If the bugs were found, or the men knew Hassan had surveillance and backup in the area, the Executioner's element of surprise would be lost. And that was just about the only advantage he and Paxton had at the moment.

Closing the car door quietly behind him, Bolan could still hear the muffled Arabic coming from the receiver inside the BMW. His guess was that there were at least twenty other men in the house with Hassan. Maybe more.

Turning away from the car, the Executioner transferred the sound-suppressed Beretta to his left hand long enough to swing the Calico out from under his *abaya*. On the other side of the vehicle, he saw Paxton fishing his own large-capacity machine pistol out of his cumbersome robelike garment.

The three-quarter moon cast an eerie half light on the fields on both sides of the road. Bolan listened to the night sounds, hearing insects buzz and an occasional bird chirp as he conducted a quick final check of the Beretta, Desert Eagle, Calico, Ka-bar fighting knife and the extra magazines for all three of his guns. On the other side of the car, he saw Paxton checking his twin .45 Commanders, his Calico, the cactus-handled dagger and other gear.

The two men met at the front of the BMW.

"Follow me, Paxton," Bolan said in a hushed voice. "We'll stay as close to the edge of the field as we can for as long as we can. But there's about a fifty-yard open area between the field and the house. We'll have to cross that fast, and we'll be highly visible with this moon."

"They may have hidden sentries somewhere, too," Paxton whispered back.

Bolan nodded in the semidarkness. "That's why we *stop* and wait when we reach the end of the field."

"Can I make a suggestion?"

"Sure," Bolan said.

"If we don't see any signs of guards, after a reasonable amount of time, let me go first."

The Executioner frowned. But before he could say anything Paxton pointed toward the Beretta in his hand. "You're the only one with a sound-suppressed weapon. And no matter how long we wait, there's always the chance we could miss a sentry—especially if they're hiding." He paused, letting it sink into the Executioner's mind. Then he finished with, "You cover me with that 93-R in case I draw one out on the way across the open area between the field and the house. That way, the men inside won't hear anything."

Bolan wasn't crazy about the idea. He had always been the kind of leader who led from the front rather than the rear.

"How about I give *you* the Beretta and you cover me while I go first?" he said.

Paxton shook his head. "It won't work for two reasons. First, you're a better shot than me. And second, I *hate* those damn Berettas. I don't care if they're the select-fire 93-R like you've got or the semiauto like the Army's gone to." He patted himself under both arms, where his twin parkerized Colt 1911 Commanders were holstered. "Stupidest damn thing the Army ever did was trade these .45s in for those Italian peashooters."

Bolan could see the unquestionable rationality in Paxton's idea. And the Executioner reminded himself that he was not working with an amateur on this mission—Brick Paxton was a U.S. Army Ranger, and a good one.

He nodded in agreement. "Go to side of the front door when you reach the house," he said. "I'll come in after you. Then we split—you go right, I'll take left, and we'll circle the house. Look into every window you possibly can. We need to know the layout, and try to determine if there are more men in other rooms."

Paxton's grin widened. "Those second-story windows are gonna be a bitch," he said. "You think we should find a way to climb up there and take a look?"

"Uh-uh," the Executioner said as they began walking back up to the top of the hill. "It looks like there's only one light on up there, and the noise we're likely to make climbing up isn't worth the risk." He pulled the Calico's bolt back to chamber the first of the fifty rounds in the cylinder drum on top of the machine pistol, then flipped the selector switch to the safe position. "We'll have to play it by ear as far as the second story goes—and probably some of the first, too. My guess is there'll be curtains or shades or both covering some, if not all, of the windows."

"Then we meet at the back of the house?" Paxton asked.

Bolan nodded. "You ready?"

Paxton nodded back.

"Then let's go."

The Executioner took off, jogging the first twenty yards or so to warm up, then breaking into a half-speed pace that would get him to the edge of the field quickly but not breathing any harder than normal. If Paxton *did* end up flushing out a sentry on his way across the open area around the house, he wanted a steady hand on the Beretta 93-R. Behind him, he could hear the Army Ranger's boots as they pattered against the packed dirt and gravel.

When they reached the end of the field, the Executioner dropped to one knee and drew the Beretta. His eyes had grown accustomed to the light of the moon and he took in the house and the rest of the area around it.

There was a small wooden porch just outside the front door, accessed by three wooden steps. But he saw no signs of sentries, guards or lookouts of any kind. That was good.

Maybe.

It could also be bad, that other part of the Executioner's brain told him. Had *he* been running an operation like this, with a potential informant being delivered to him, he'd have definitely posted men outside to look for surveillance. Ali and his Hands of Allah people were either half-trained incompetents—which wasn't out of the question these days—or something else was wrong. Something that had begun eating away at Bolan for some time now.

Exactly which side *was* Abdul Hassan on? he wondered. Was he truly risking his life to help them, or was he drawing them into a trap to get them killed?

Bolan glanced at his watch. He had lost all contact with Hassan by leaving the receiver in the BMW, and if the man was on the level, by now he might be tied to a chair and getting his fingernails pulled out with a set of pliers. So Bolan gave himself only one minute to survey the area around the house before he turned around toward Paxton. "You ready to go?" he whispered.

The Army Ranger's head bobbed up and down. He moved around the Executioner and, in the bright moonlight, Bolan could see he held the cactus-handled Damascus dagger in his right hand.

Bolan nodded to himself. Paxton might be letting his emotions get in the way of doing his job now and then, but he was a brave warrior—there was no arguing that. If he came across a lookout himself on his way to the house, he was obviously willing to take his chances with a four-inch blade rather than shoot one of his .45s or the 9 mm Calico and alert the men inside.

Luckily, it turned out that he didn't need the knife *or* a gun. Bolan watched the man sprint toward the front of the house, crouching low. At the same time, still using his night-vision goggles, the Executioner continued to search the yard area for any sign of movement. None came.

If there were any sentries posted outside, they were waiting.

As soon as Paxton had dropped down next to the front porch, Bolan followed him, the Beretta gripped in his right hand. At this point, he still wanted silence if he had to shoot.

The time for the roar of the Desert Eagle, and the sputtering full-auto rounds from the Calico, was yet to come.

But come it would, the Executioner knew.

And soon.

THE HOUSE WAS NOT the usual Dutch-style structure that looked as if it had come straight off of a Netherlands postcard. Whoever had built the house years ago—and Brick Paxton didn't think for a minute that it had been the men who occupied it now—must have been fans of the American West. The house appeared to have come from one of the many American companies who put together modular log cabin packages and shipped them all over the world, as well as within the United States. The logs had been flattened on the outside rather than left rounded, and were held together, it appeared, with some sort of gray chinking. Most of the gray had been painted brown to look like dried mud or sod, but as he began to circle the house, staying low beneath the windows, Paxton could see spots where the paint had worn away and the gray shone through in the moonlight.

Only a small porch—accessed by climbing three rough cedar steps—stood on the ground floor in front of the door. But the second story appeared to have an outside porch that ran completely around the house. He could imagine the Hands of Allah terrorists sitting outside at night, looking up at the stars, perhaps drinking coffee and talking in hushed voices. In this log cabin, they would not be much different than Americans at a lake or mountain retreat spending a quiet evening.

Except for the fact that they'd be planning bombings, kidnappings and murders each evening rather than talking about how good dinner had been or yawning and pointing out how you got sleepier much earlier in such a relaxed atmosphere.

The Army Ranger moved away from the steps. The first darkened window he came to had the shade drawn tightly, and he was unable to see anything inside—even though the light in the room was on. Knowing he would learn nothing there, he took a deep breath, gripped the dagger that Phil had given him for his birthday a little tighter in his fist and peered slowly around the corner of the house. Seeing no one on this side, either, he turned the corner and moved on toward the next window.

The shade had been pulled down here, as well, but one corner bent slightly outward, and the light was on. Taking his time, he slowly raised his head until one eye peered over the windowsill. He could see only part of what appeared to be a bedroom. But what really caught his eye was the two legs he could see, extending off the side of the bed. Whoever was sitting there, the rest of him hidden by the shade, was wearing desert tan BDU pants and black leather and nylon combat boots not unlike those on Paxton's own feet. The barrel of a rifle-obviously resting across the man's lap—was also visible. It appeared to be one of the Kalashnikov series of rifles, probably either an AK-47 or that battle-proved weapon's next generation, the AK-74.

But whatever it was, and whoever it was sitting on the bed, wasn't any Dutch tulip farmer.

Paxton moved on, wondering for a moment what Cooper was discovering on his side of the house. Only a fool would believe "Cooper" was his real name, but that didn't matter. Brick Paxton understood the need-to-know philosophy as well as any soldier, and he didn't need to know the man's real name to realize that "Cooper" was undoubtedly the finest warrior he had ever worked with. The man was big and immensely strong, but his size didn't seem to affect the catlike reflexes and mind-numbing speed he'd exhibited in battle so far. And smart, damn smart, Paxton thought.

At first, Brick Paxton remembered as he came to the next lighted window, he had resented being teamed up with the man. He was more used to giving orders than taking them, and he had doubted that Cooper would be anything but a nuisance on this mission. He had even planned on challenging the big man to a little one-on-one unarmed combat after they'd arrived in Amsterdam and settled into their hotel, just to show him who would be running the show. But by that time, Cooper had almost single-handedly taken out the hijackers on the 747 and saved the lives of all the people on board.

As far as Brick Paxton was concerned, Cooper didn't need to prove himself beyond that. And the Army Ranger was damn glad he hadn't had to challenge the man, too. He now had no doubt about who would have walked away from such a contest the winner.

Rising again, Paxton quickly glanced into the window. It was smaller than the others, higher up the wall and—as he'd expected—led into a bathroom. Seated on the toilet, his BDU pants down around his ankles, was a hard-looking, dark-skinned man. In his hands were the open pages of a newspaper. Paxton was too far away to see the print, but when the man turned the page from left to right instead of right to left, he assumed it must be some Arabic publication.

There was nothing odd about a man using the restroom, or reading a newspaper while he did so. But it struck the Army Ranger as a little unusual that while he answered nature's call, the man on the toilet had another AK—this one definitely an AK-47, leaning against the wall next to him. And on the belt at the top of his pants on the floor, Paxton could see a Russian Tokarev pistol, extra magazines and various other items of battle.

Abdul Hassan had definitely *not* been brought to Koran study session, as he'd first been told.

The last window on the side of the house was dark and had curtains pulled over it. Paxton could see nothing, so after another quick glance around the corner to the back, he stepped around again.

And as he did, a figure rose up out of the darkness.

The man—who had been almost invisible, sitting in the shadows—held an American-made M-16 in his hands as he rose. As always happened during moments of life-and-death combat, thoughts raced through Brick Paxton's brain at the speed of light.

Where had the man gotten the M-16—what American had he killed and taken it from? How had he missed the man when he peered around the corner?

Why hadn't the man moved on him earlier?

Had he been asleep at his post and awakened by some noise Paxton had made?

Those thoughts just came and went, unanswered because at the moment they were irrelevant.

All that really mattered at this place and time was that this man had to be silenced before he could pull the trigger of the M-16, kill Brick Paxton, and sound the alarm to the men inside the house.

Paxton had been holding the cactus-handled dagger low and to his side. Now, instinctively, from countless hours of training, he brought the Damascus blade upward, his thoughts once more racing through his brain. He knew the four-inch blade wouldn't be long enough to penetrate the heavy BDU coat the man wore, and then continue far enough into the heart to do immediate damage. So the Army Ranger reached forward, grabbing the barrel of the American made rifle with his left hand, then circled his knife hand out to the side before driving it into the trigger guard behind the trigger. He could feel the pressure as the terrorist tried to pull the trigger back.

But it was blocked by the thin point of the blade.

At the same time Paxton leaned forward, driving the hairline of his head into the nose of the terrorist. Then he jammed the dagger even farther into the trigger guard before twisted it up and around until he felt the razor-sharp edge meet flesh. Slicing back with all of the strength in his hand and arm, he severed the terrorist's trigger finger.

The finger dropped to the ground as blood spurted from the stump.

Paxton's head strike had knocked the man backward a half

step, but the Ranger had moved with him, still clutching the barrel of the M-16. With the threat of loud 5.56 mm rounds alerting the men inside that they were under attack no longer an issue, Paxton took his time as he pulled the dagger back out of the trigger guard and drove it into the center of the man's throat.

As soon as he felt the blade halt at the hilt, he ripped to his right, severing the jugular.

Paxton stepped to the side to avoid the spray of red that now came from the man's neck as the guard fell forward onto the cold hard ground. The Hands of Allah terrorist was still sputtering when a dark figure appeared in the corner of Paxton's eye. The Ranger turned, the dagger in front of him, ready to fight again.

But he didn't have to. Hanging at the end of the arm of the dark figure, he saw the distinctive outline of a Beretta 93-R.

Bolan moved up next to him. "Where'd he come from?" he whispered.

Paxton shrugged in the semilight. "I don't know," he said. "He just...*appeared.* My guess is he was out here and fell into a light sleep. I probably woke him up as I got close."

Bolan nodded. "It doesn't matter," he said. "You see anything useful?"

"In the corner bedroom, front of the house," Paxton whispered back. "There's at least one man in BDUs with a rifle across his lap. And there's another one dressed in battle gear with an AK-47 taking a dump in the bathroom."

In the light of the three-quarters moon, it was easy for Paxton to see Bolan frown. "Both men had their rifles ready?"

"Looked like it to me," Paxton answered.

"That goes right along with what I saw. I got a glimpse into the front room. Every man in there is *holding* a rifle. They don't have them resting against the wall, or even slung over their backs. They've got them *ready.*"

"What about Abdul?" Paxton asked.

"I could only see part of his back. But he's still standing in the middle of the group, and it looks to me like he's still arguing with them."

"You'd think by now they'd have started beating him or something."

"Yeah, you would, wouldn't you?" Bolan said. "Something's very strange about this situation." He paused, looked over his shoulder, then said, "Follow me back around to where I could see inside. I could also hear them from there. Maybe you can pick up on what's going on."

The big man turned his back and Paxton followed. The window to which Bolan led him looked into what appeared to be the living room. A large-screen TV was angled outward from one corner, and couches and chairs were scattered around the room. Wooden venetian blinds covered the large picture window, but they were old and warped and gaped open enough to see inside in several places.

Both Paxton and Bolan knelt, looking through the holes. Paxton found himself frowning as he listened. While one of the men inside held a rifle barrel to Hassan's throat, a dozen voices—including that of their informant—spit out angry-sounding Arabic. Again, it was too fast for the Army Ranger to pick it all up. He got enough, however, to realize they were still arguing about whether Hassan was really on their side.

But there was another weird, out-of-place sight he could see through the slats. Some of the men—even those who were speaking angrily—were *smiling*.

Motioning with his hand for Bolan to follow him, Paxton led the big man around to the side of the house. "It's the same argument as before," he said. "And again, I couldn't pick it all up. But…I don't know exactly how to explain it…there's a *feeling* I got from it all."

"Just explain it as best you can," Bolan said.

"Well," said Paxton, "it's like it kind of sounded phony. Or rehearsed. Like some bad high-school play or something. And a couple of them are even smiling."

"I saw that, too," said the Executioner.

"They're repeating themselves over and over," Paxton went on. "Still saying pretty much the same things we heard when we were still in the car."

"I think the key to it all is that it's been going on at this level far too long," Bolan said. "By now, they should have either killed him or begun torturing him."

"You think he's working against us?" Paxton asked, knowing Bolan had to have thought of the same possibility.

"At this point, I don't know. But did you notice that besides the guys who were smiling, several of the men inside seemed as interested in the doors and windows as they were in Abdul?"

"Yeah. A couple kept glancing that way."

"They're expecting someone. It may be that they just figure Abdul would have had a surveillance team with him. Or maybe they've found the bugs I taped to him and are forcing him to play along to set us up."

"There's only one way to find out, isn't there?" Paxton said.

"That's right," Bolan said. "I'll take the front. You take the back. Take out the guy you saw in the bedroom and the one on the john first, then join me in the living room. As soon as we've cleared the ground floor, we'll move upstairs."

Bolan raised his arm toward his eyes and looked at his watch. "Check your timepiece," he told the Army Ranger. "We kick the doors in thirty seconds starting…now."

Paxton took off, jogging around the house to the back again. In the moonlight, he could still see the terrorist he had killed with the short-bladed dagger his brother had given him. *That one was for you, Phil*, he thought as he sheathed the blade and pulled his Calico 950 out to the end of its sling. *And there are about to be a lot more.*

The Army Ranger glanced at his watch. In ten more seconds, all hell was going to break loose. Noise wouldn't matter then. Moving to the back door, he counted down the final five seconds under his breath, then shot a boot out and against the wood just below the knob.

At the same time, he heard gunfire erupt at the front of the house.

BOLAN WATCHED the second hand pass the thirty-second mark on the luminous numerals of his watch, then kicked the front door.

The solid oak plank not only opened, but it also flew back off the hinges, taking most of the frame on both sides of the log house with it as it sailed inside.

The Executioner was a mere half step behind the flying wood as he swung the Calico up to the end of its sling and flipped the selector switch to full-auto. He found himself in a short, unoccupied entryway, but only a few feet away he could hear the voices that had been speaking suddenly quiet.

Before anyone could recover from their shock and speak again, he had jumped over the door, crossed the hallway and stepped into a large living area.

At least twenty men stood around the room, just now beginning to recover from the shock of the door exploding, and trying to bring the rifles in their hands into play. They had been ready for intruders—that had been obvious. What they had *not* counted on was the lightning speed with which their enemy would come.

A steel spiral staircase leading toward the second floor stood just to the Executioner's side as he stopped at the edge of the room. From where he stood he could see Abdul Hassan in the center of the group, facing him. The man's robe had been pulled open and both the Nagra recorder and transmitter ripped from his chest and back. A tall man with a beard at least a foot long stood next to him, holding both devices in one hand. Long strips of white adhesive tape—covered in hair from Hassan's chest and back as Bolan had predicted—hung toward the floor.

In his other hand the bearded terrorist gripped a pistol.

The Executioner aimed the Calico and pulled the trigger back. Five lightning-fast 9 mm rounds flew from the barrel of the machine pistol before he let up again. The semijacketed hollowpoints created parts in the long chin whiskers as they passed through them into the man's chest, and the odor of burning hair mixed with the cordite filled the air.

Bolan pulled the Calico past Hassan, taking aim at the man closest to him on the informant's other side. Before he could bring his assault rifle to bear, Bolan sent a 5-round burst into his chest. As the terrorist dropped, Hassan dived to the floor and rolled out of sight behind a couch. The informant didn't look as if he'd been hit—he was just doing his best to get out of the line of fire.

With the living room now free of potential collateral damage, the Executioner took full advantage of the high-capacity, fast-shooting Calico machine pistol. He held the trigger back, and round after round spewed out of the barrel as the hot brass dropped straight down from the weapon's ejection port. Three more men fell to Bolan's assault before they could react.

But by now, the rest of the Hands of Allah men were getting their rifles and other weapons into play, which meant the Executioner had to move, or suffer the return fire that was about to come his way.

Diving forward, Bolan rolled behind a stuffed armchair,

then came up on one knee as 7.62 mm NATO rounds exploded from an AK-47 a mere foot away from him. Aiming up and over the arm of the chair, he fired again, this time centering four more rounds in the middle of the chest of a huge Arab wearing an OD green T-shirt and fatigue pants. The Soviet rifle fell to the floor and the big man fell over it.

In between his own gunfire and that of the Hands of Allah, the Executioner heard 9 mm explosions coming from the rear of the house. Good—Paxton was taking out the man on the toilet and the one in the bedroom. Maybe even more they hadn't been able to see through the windows. In any case, the Ranger was on his way. And when he got to the living room, with all of the attention focused on the Executioner, Paxton should be able to take out several of the enemy before they even realized a rear assault was in progress.

The Executioner ducked as lighter rounds came at him. They sounded more like 5.56 mm rounds, which meant the weapon was most likely an AK-74 or an M-16. The small-caliber, high-velocity bullets ripped through the arm of the chair-exactly where the Executioner's head had been only a second before.

Scrambling behind the chair, Bolan leaned around the other side and brought the Calico into play once again.

This time, the man firing at him was reed thin. But that didn't make him any less deadly—not as long as he had the strength to pull a trigger. Which he did, and tried to do again as he swung his rifle Bolan's way as soon as the Executioner's head popped back up into sight.

Bolan was a second faster, and another five rounds stitched their way up the man's chest to his throat and finally into his face. He toppled backward, and collapsed to the floor.

Suddenly a weapon that sounded almost identical to Bolan's own began popping out rounds from the other side of the room. The Executioner glanced that way and saw that Paxton had finally reached the living room. Firing his own Calico on full-auto, he took down three of the remaining men with bullets in the back before they even knew he was there.

The direction from which this new fire came now drew the attention of the other men, and Bolan took full advantage of their surprise. Having caught them in a cross fire, he rose higher and saw a tall, turbaned man in a white T-shirt and baggy jeans racking the slide of a 12-gauge riot shotgun.

The Calico came up.

The turban went down.

The Executioner swung his machine pistol to the left, pulling back on the trigger once more and cutting figure eights through the air across the remaining men. Four more of the Hands of Allah terrorists fell to 9 mm hollowpoints, blood, flesh and chips of bone flying through the air almost as if a hand grenade had exploded at their feet.

Only four terrorists were still on their feet. Bolan trained the barrel of his Calico on one of the men who had a drooping mustache much longer than his short beard. A quintet of 9 mm rounds struck the man in the face, and he toppled to the wooden floor almost headless.

Bolan had not been able to keep an exact count on the rounds he'd fired so far, but he knew the 50-round drum had to be nearly empty. Snapping the drum off the top of the Calico, he reached under his left arm, past the Beretta, and ripped open the Velcro retainer holding the 100-round drum in place. A moment later, it was on top of the gun and the near empty 50-rounder had taken its place in the DeSantis carry rig.

In the corner of his eye, Bolan saw Paxton. The Army Ranger held his Calico in both hands as he triggered a full stream of autofire into a chubby terrorist who seemed to have frozen in place with fear.

But as they took these two men down, the other pair of surviving terrorists ducked through an archway that led to what looked like a dining room to the Executioner's left. Before either Bolan or Paxton could fire, they moved to the side of the archway, out of sight, behind the walls.

Bolan rose to full height now and swept the Calico back and forth across the room, making sure none of the "dead" were coming back to life. He was about to call out to Paxton to begin checking the rest of the rooms on his side of the house when a tiny glint of stainless steel flickered behind the Ranger.

The Executioner swung his machine pistol that way, and to Paxton it looked as if the Executioner was aiming at *him*. The Army Ranger's brow furrowed, his mouth dropped open and his eyes widened in confusion as Bolan pulled the trigger.

A second later, another terrorist fell forward in the hallway behind Paxton. A nickel-plated revolver of some kind skidded across the wooden floor, and the expression on Paxton's face changed to one of gratitude.

With this sudden break in the carnage, the Army Ranger took one hand away from his gun, threw a quick and sloppy salute Bolan's way and mouthed, "Thanks."

Bolan nodded in return, then pointed toward the rooms along the wall closest to Paxton. The Ranger started toward the closest door as Bolan moved toward the open archway where the remaining men from the living room had disappeared. As he passed the couch, he whispered, "Abdul! Are you hit?"

"No," the informant said from somewhere on the other side of the couch.

Bolan had spoken softly, hoping to keep from giving his position away to the men on the other side of the archway.

He wasn't that lucky.

An arm holding a blue-worn 1911 Government Model

suddenly reached out into the archway and fired. The shot was hurried and missed the Executioner by at least three feet.

Bolan could almost feel himself smiling as he aimed just to the side of the arm. The outside of the house might have been built from logs but nothing but drywall stood between him and the man who had just fired the Colt. The Executioner's full-auto stream penetrated the thin barrier as if it hadn't even been there. Round after round pumped through the drywall, and white dust and chips flew up in the air like a sudden indoor snowstorm before floating back toward the wooden floor.

By the time he let up on the trigger, a hole the size of a basketball had been shot out of the wall, and Bolan could see the dead man lying on the floor in the other room.

At least he *looked* dead. The Executioner had not survived over the years by taking unnecessary chances, and he kept the Calico up and ready in front of him as he moved cautiously toward the archway. Besides, he had seen two men retreat into the adjoining room. There was at least one Hands of Allah man still alive, and armed, on the other side of what was left of the wall. There might even be more, if they'd been in that room, out of sight, when the gunfight had started.

Just as he reached the archway, Bolan heard the sound of more rounds spitting from Paxton's Calico. The Army Ranger had found a stray himself, it seemed.

Just before he reached the archway, the Executioner dropped to the floor on his belly. Using his elbows to pull himself forward, he crawled across the last few feet until he could see into the room.

The other terrorist who had made his brief escape from the living room stood in the corner next to a small television set on a table. He had his AK-47 against his shoulder and aimed at the opening but, as the Executioner had suspected, the weapon—and his vision—was trained at eye level.

He *saw* Bolan as soon as the Executioner appeared in the archway. But the second it took for him to correct his point of aim signed his own death warrant.

Bracing himself on his left elbow, the Executioner shot the Calico one-handed, letting a good half-dozen 9 mm slugs drill through the khaki BDU blouse the man wore. Before the terrorist could hit the floor, however, Bolan was back on his feet and sweeping the Calico back and forth again, checking for any other terrorists in the room. There was none.

The room looked as if a bomb had exploded in it. Men lay dead on the couches and chairs, and blood ran across the hardwood floor, settling in the cracks between the slats. The Executioner stepped over several bodies to where Abdul Hassan had risen to a sitting position on the floor. "Anybody upstairs?" he asked the informant.

Hassan shrugged. "I wouldn't know," he said. "I never got past this room."

"Stay where you are," Bolan ordered as he started to go check on Paxton's progress.

"But what if more of them arrive?" Hassan said, pointing at a window. "I will need a gun to protect myself."

The Executioner looked over his shoulder and swept the Calico across the room. "I don't think you'll have much trouble finding one," he said. "Take your pick." He forced a smile at Hassan as he walked on. It was a smile he didn't feel but it gave him an excuse to keep from turning his back on the man as he made his way toward the bedrooms where Paxton had gone.

Something smelled rotten in this deal. Whether Abdul had led them into a trap at this remote log cabin remained to be seen. But until he was certain, the Executioner was taking no chances.

Bolan found Paxton in the front bedroom, just about to open a closet door. They nodded at each other, then the Army

Ranger let his machine pistol drop to the end of his arm as he grasped the knob with the other hand. Bolan raised his Calico and aimed it at the closet as the door came open with Paxton moving to the side, out of the line of fire.

The closet was empty.

"You've cleared this whole side?" the Executioner asked the Ranger.

Paxton nodded.

"Then it's time to head upstairs," said Bolan. "I don't know if we can do it or not, but if we can, I'd like to take at least one of these scumbags alive for questioning."

Paxton nodded his understanding. "If we don't, we're no closer to finding Phil than we were before we even came out here." He paused for a second, looked toward the door, then dropped his voice to a whisper. "What's Abdul's condition?"

"He's fine," the Executioner whispered back. "I told him to stay in the living room. He was worried about other terrorists coming to the house while we were upstairs so he's acquisitioning one of the dead men's weapons."

"You think he set us up?" Paxton asked, his voice still low.

"To tell you the truth," Bolan said. "I don't know. I don't know if you got there in time to see it or not, but they'd found the Nagra and transmitter by the time I kicked in the front door. They could have been forcing him to play along to sucker us in. We'll ask him when this is over."

"And we'll either get the truth or a lie," Paxton said.

"Right," Bolan said as he started out the door again. "But sooner or later, one way or another, we'll get the truth." Hurrying back to the living room, he shrugged out of his *abaya* and *kaffiyeh* and adjusted his weapons and the other equipment on his blacksuit. Behind him, Paxton did the same.

The sharp-angled, wickedly twisting spiral staircase presented a dangerous ascent, but as far as the Executioner could see, it was the only way upstairs. So, reconnecting the Calico to the sling, he let the 100-round magazine hang awkwardly at his side and drew the Desert Eagle. Then he turned his back to the steps.

"Cover me," he ordered Paxton.

U.S. Army Rangers were as well-trained in house clearing as the finest SWAT teams, and Paxton knew exactly what to do. He aimed his Calico toward the second floor and waited as the Executioner began backing up the stairs, the Desert Eagle in both hands above his head.

Bolan moved quickly but carefully, knowing that too slow made him an easy target and too fast might make him miss some tiny sight or movement that could save his life. His guess was that there were more bedrooms upstairs, and the fact that no one had been sleeping in either of the downstairs beds made it even more likely that a whole shift of terrorists might have been asleep on the second story when the shooting started.

But if they *had* been asleep, they wouldn't be now. Not with the hundreds of rounds that had exploded in the past five minutes right below them.

The Executioner was somewhat surprised when he reached the top step without meeting any resistance. But then, as he took the last step and backed out onto the open hall that led around the entire upper floor, he heard a door open behind him.

A man with crazed eyes wearing nothing but white shorts and brandishing a sword sprinted out of the doorway in a suicide mission. The Executioner sent a lone .44 Magnum round into the center of his chest, then stepped to the side to let the man's own force throw him over the railing. The terrorist landed next to Paxton, on top of one of the other terrorists who'd died earlier.

Bolan's eyes raked the hallway. Several more doors—all closed—led into more bedrooms. When they had all stayed closed for thirty seconds, the Executioner looked down and motioned Paxton on up.

With Bolan covering him from a more advantageous angle, the Army Ranger sprinted up the steps. A moment later, he was at the Executioner's side.

"We'll work as a team," Bolan whispered. "I go into each room while you stay outside as cover and backup."

Bolan started with the room the man with the sword had just exited. He looked under the bed, then into the closet, but found no one. Opening the door to the upstairs porch, he had no better luck there. When he had come out of the room again, he said to Paxton, "Remember—we want one alive if possible."

Paxton nodded as Bolan approached he next room on the second floor. It too was empty, as were all the other bedrooms and upper porches on the log cabin's second story.

It seemed that all of the Hands of Allah but the man with the sword had come downstairs for the arrival of Ali and Abdul Hassan.

When he had cleared the last room, Bolan motioned Paxton inside. Keeping his voice down so that Hassan wouldn't hear him below, he said, "We're back to square one again. Nobody alive to lead us on to your brother."

"You want to know what I think?" the Army Ranger asked. His face was bright red with anger. "I think that little son of a bitch downstairs set us up. And I think I'll go downstairs, beat all of the information out of him I can, then put a bullet in his head." He turned quickly back toward the door.

Bolan reached out, catching his arm. "Wait," he said. "There's a better way to do this."

The Executioner explained his idea and, as he spoke, he watched Brick Paxton cool down in stages. By the time Bolan finished speaking, it appeared that the Ranger's outburst of frustration was over. He didn't smile, but he didn't frown or grimace, either. "Okay," Paxton agreed in a low voice. "What you're saying makes sense."

Bolan holstered the Desert Eagle and took his Calico off the sling again. He led the way down the spiral staircase. Hassan was waiting behind the couch in the living room. The informant had picked up one of the AK-47s and jerked it toward them when he heard them approach.

Both Bolan and Paxton instinctively raised their Calicos and aimed them back at the man. Then, slowly, his whole body shivering with the movement, Hassan lowered his weapon. "I am sorry," the informant said. "I did not know it was you." In a trembling voice an octave higher than normal, he asked, "Everyone else is dead?"

Bolan and Paxton let the Calicos drop to the end of their slings, but the Executioner kept his finger inside the trigger guard as he nodded. If Hassan was playing both sides against the middle and had led them to this log cabin as a trap, why hadn't he just shot them both now? Maybe he was afraid he couldn't kill them both before one of them got him.

Or maybe he wasn't dirty after all. Sometimes, coincidences really did occur and could distort the overall picture of a mission.

The bottom line was that, at this point, Bolan couldn't be sure if Hassan was really with them, or against them.

But he knew how to find out.

"Yeah," he answered the informant. "They're all dead. We're back where we started again."

Hassan dropped the AK-47 to the floor. "I am sorry," he said again. "They found the recorder and transmitter. Then they held me at gun point and forced me to lure you in." He lowered his head and stared at the bloody wooden floor around his feet. "There was nothing else I could do. But now I am ashamed of myself."

It was exactly what the Executioner had expected to hear. Whether it was true or not remained to be seen.

"Let's go," Bolan said. "We'll regroup and come up with another plan back at the hotel."

With nothing positive to show for all their efforts, the three men left the log cabin and walked back past the field to the BMW.

9

The sun was rising again by the time the BMW returned to the Hotel Amstel in Amsterdam. "Same as before," Bolan said as he parked down the block along the street. "We take different entrances and elevators and meet upstairs at the suite."

Like Bolan, Paxton was wearing his trench coat over his blacksuit again. He nodded from the passenger's seat. Hassan, again dressed in his blue blazer and white turban, did the same from behind him. Bolan had picked up the Nagra recorder and transmitter from the floor back at the log cabin and, along with the homing device Hassan had worn in the tail of his *kaffiyeh,* returned them to one of their equipment bags. Now the three men lifted the bags out of the backseat, got out of the vehicle and took off in separate directions.

Ten minutes later, they were seated around the coffee table in the suite's living room again.

"I am sorry for what I was forced to do last night," Hassan said, his face a mask of shame. "I am a coward."

Bolan didn't know if the words were sincere or not, but at this point, he was still playing along with the man as if he believed him. He shook his head. "Don't worry about it," he said. "You didn't have any choice. Besides, you gave us plenty of warning by speaking in English as much as you did."

"I did *try,*" Hassan said, looking up. He cleared his throat, then said, "There is one other place to which I could go. Another coffeehouse." He glanced at his wristwatch. "But the people it would benefit me to speak to will not be there for several hours."

"What time do you figure they might arrive?" Bolan asked.

"Not before noon at the earliest. Late afternoon is more likely."

"That's okay," said the Executioner. "We could all use a little sleep before we go into action again anyway." He cleared his throat. "Exactly where *is* this coffeehouse?"

"It is not in any of the Arabic settlements," Hassan answered. "In fact, it is only a couple of blocks from here. It is located next to an old castle that has been allowed to deteriorate for many years."

Bolan nodded. "Then let's take a catnap." He leaned back in his chair and closed his eyes but continued speaking. "You two take whichever bedrooms you want. I'll be fine right here." He lifted his eyelids just enough to see Paxton head off toward one of the bedrooms while Hassan stood up and walked toward the other.

The truth was, Bolan had no intention of sleeping. Not with Abdul being the wild card he was at the moment. The Executioner planned to stay awake with his eyes and ears sharp to see if the informant tried to make contact with anyone either with his cell phone, the room phone or by leaving while he believed Bolan and Paxton to be asleep.

Thirty minutes later, the Executioner could hear loud snores coming from the bedroom Paxton had taken. He got up and moved quietly across the carpet, closing the door. The way the suite was laid out, he knew that Hassan could see his movements through his own open door, and the logical thing for the informant to believe was that the Executioner found the snoring irritating. It also gave Bolan an excuse to look into Hassan's room after he'd turned and started back toward his chair.

The informant had taken off his blue blazer and turban and lay on his side, facing away from the Executioner. Whether he was asleep or not, Bolan had no way of knowing, but he guessed by the rhythmic movements of his chest that he was. So this was as good a time as any to implement the plan that would tell them exactly where Hassan's loyalties lay.

Bolan moved swiftly and silently toward the equipment bags that held the robes the men had worn. Digging through the garments, he found Hassan's headdress—the one he had worn in the other coffeehouses and would undoubtedly wear again when he went looking for more radical Muslim terrorists later that afternoon. He kept a close eye on the open door to Hassan's room as he dug through another bag.

The homing device Hassan had worn in the tail of the *kaffiyeh* earlier was large enough that any man wearing it in his headdress would notice the weight. It had to be to provide the long-range signals Bolan had suspected they might need the night before. And besides, Hassan had already *known* he'd be wearing it.

What Bolan wanted now was a tracking device the informant wouldn't notice. He wanted Abdul Hassan to believe he was free and on his own when he went out again that afternoon.

In the other bag, the Executioner found exactly what he'd been looking for—an experimental device the Stony Man Farm's experts had been perfecting for the past several months. In a small plastic envelope was what looked like a U.S. postage stamp. He pulled out the sticker, peeled off the back to expose a sticky side and pressed the device onto the inside of the wooden ring that held Hassan's *kaffiyeh* in place. But the sight made him frown. The igal was made of dark brown wood, and the "stamp" stood out in bold relief. Besides that, it was too wide and the sides curled over the top and bottom of the wood.

There was no way Hassan would miss it when he put it on.

Hiding the *igal* back in the bag, the Executioner pulled his cell phone from a pocket of his blacksuit and walked past the informant's bedroom. The man had not changed positions, and still appeared to be asleep. But the Executioner was taking no chances.

Entering the bathroom, Bolan closed and locked the door behind him, then turned on the shower. After the signal went through a series of security cutouts, he had Barbara Price on the line.

"Hello, Striker," she said.

"I need the Bear," Bolan told her.

Price was too professional to even bother answering. Bolan heard a click and a second later Aaron Kurtzman was on the line. "What can I do for you, big guy?" he asked.

"I'm about to try out that postage-stamp homing device you and Gadgets have been working on. It *will* work, won't it?"

"Yep," Kurtzman said. "It'll show up on the maps I programmed into your laptop, and it's even more precise than the larger model. Only kink we haven't straightened out yet is its limited range."

"*How* limited?" Bolan asked.

"You gonna be in the city or out in the boonies without other radio transmissions getting in the way?"

"We're almost right in the center of Amsterdam."

"Then you'd better stay within half a mile," Kurtzman said. "Sorry about that."

"Half a mile should be enough," the Executioner said. "Now, one other thing." He told the computer wizard about how the stamp stood out on the *igal*.

"Just cut off the sides of the stamp where they curl over

the *igal*," Kurtzman said. "The homer's a microchip right in the center. It shouldn't affect anything at all."

"How about the stamp itself? The bright colors against the wood—"

"You got a permanent marking pen of some kind?" Kurtzman interrupted.

"Yeah," Bolan said.

"Then just color over the stamp face. That won't affect anything, either."

"Thanks, Bear," the Executioner said. "You've made my day."

"That's why they pay me the big bucks," Kurtzman said, chuckling as he hung up.

Hassan was still sleeping on his side when Bolan returned to the baggage. Pulling the *igal* out again, he found a black felt marker in his briefcase and carefully colored in the stamp. When he was finished, it was almost the same shade as the dark wooden ring. Using the Ka-bar, he trimmed the edges. When he was finished, he could barely see the transmitter himself.

Unless he was looking for it—which Hassan wouldn't be—the informant wasn't going to see it when he got dressed in a few hours.

Bolan returned to his chair and allowed himself to drift into a half doze in which he was still aware of everything going on around him. It was a talent he'd developed over the years, and it rested him almost as well as a proper nap. There was nothing to do now but wait.

One hour went by. Then two. Paxton continued to snore through the door, but Hassan's bedroom remained silent. Thirty minutes later, the Executioner sensed movement.

He got up out of his chair and walked to the open door to the informant's room. The man had his cellular phone in his hand and was letting it warm up.

"What are you doing?" Bolan asked in the friendliest voice he could muster.

"I woke up *famished,*" Hassan said. "I was calling room service."

"It'd be a lot easier doing that on the room phone," Bolan said, glancing to the instrument on the stand next to the bed.

Hassan looked that way and snorted. "I am still half asleep, I guess," he said. "You're right." He closed his phone and stuck it back into the pocket of his khaki slacks.

Before he could reach for the room phone, however, Bolan said, "I'm hungry, too. But there's no sense in taking the chance on waking McBride up when they deliver our order. Let me change out of this blacksuit and we'll go downstairs to one of the restaurants."

Hassan nodded his understanding. And if he was disappointed that his call had been canceled, his face didn't show it.

The informant took a seat in the living room while Bolan got back into his jeans, a black sweater and the brown suede safari vest with the Desert Eagle, Beretta, knife and other equipment hidden beneath it. Quietly, so as not to awaken Paxton, the two men left and took an elevator down to the main floor.

In the first restaurant they came to—more of a café, actually—they both ordered club sandwiches with another to take back to Paxton when he woke up. Thirty minutes later, they were back in the suite.

Bolan looked at his watch. "We've still got another couple of hours to kill," he said. "Let's go back to sleep."

Hassan nodded and disappeared into his bedroom again. Bolan returned to his chair.

An hour later, the Executioner heard the faint sounds of footsteps on the carpet. He had his eyes half closed when he saw Hassan appear again, headed for the door to the hall.

Bolan waited until the man had grasped the doorknob to say, "Where are you going, Abdul?"

The informant whirled like a kid caught with his hand in the cookie jar. "I am sorry," he said. "I was trying not to awaken you. I am still hungry. Sometimes when I am under stress, I eat too much."

The Executioner forced another in a long series of insincere smiles at Hassan. "Hold on," he said. He got up, went back to where their bags were sitting in the corner of the living room, unzipped one and pulled out three granola bars. Tossing them across the room to Hassan, he said, "Here—this should hold you over. The less we get seen in the hotel from now on, the better. Word of what happened at the log cabin has to have gotten back to Hands of Allah faction holding the hostages by now, and we already pushed our luck when we went downstairs earlier."

Abdul caught the granola bars, one by one, and smiled. Whether his smile was any more genuine than Bolan's, the Executioner couldn't know. But the man thanked him and disappeared back into the bedroom.

The Executioner sat back and listened as Hassan unwrapped and ate the three granola bars in the other room. Then a soft snore began to come from his room, as well as Paxton's. Bolan gave it another hour and a half, then looked down at his watch. It was now two-thirty in the afternoon. Everyone should be rested, and the radicals in the next coffeehouse should be there if they were going.

Bolan awakened Paxton first, telling him quickly in hushed tones about how Hassan had tried to make outside contact while he thought Bolan and the Ranger slept. He also clued him in concerning the postage-stamp homing device in the *igal.*

"If we didn't need him," Paxton whispered when he'd heard the story, "I'd cut his throat right now."

"I know it sounds like he's guilty," said Bolan, "but we've got to be sure. He's wanting to make contact with someone, it looks like. The postage stamp will tell us if he really goes to the coffeehouse or someplace else."

Paxton had slept in his blacksuit, simply taking his Colt Commanders and other gear off and placing them on the bed beside him. Now, he began reholstering and reequipping as Bolan left to wake Hassan. The man really was asleep, which surprised the Executioner. Despite the arrows pointing toward Hassan's guilt, there were other arrows pointing away from it, too.

When the three men met in the living room again, Hassan went immediately to the equipment bags, found his *igal* and placed it on his head. He exhibited no sign whatsoever that he'd seen the dark sticker inside the wooden ring. He turned to the Executioner. "Do you have the homing device?" he asked.

"I've got it," Bolan said, "but I don't think it's wise to use it this time. Or the recorder or transmitter. The Hands of Allah are obviously used to checking for wires. So I'd say we're better off just letting you run free. Come back to the suite as soon as you've learned anything, and we'll plan from there."

Hassan couldn't, or maybe didn't try, to hide the look of relief that came over his face. "Along with the hostages, of course," he said. "News of what happened at the cabin will be the main topic of conversation. People will know that *someone* had to lead the men who killed everyone at the log cabin to that spot. Everyone will be suspect—especially a new face such as mine." He paused a second, then said, "So I agree with your decision. Anyone I talk to in the coffeehouse is likely to check me for wires."

Bolan nodded. "We'll stay here and wait on you."

Hassan gave him a short, courteous bow, then slipped into his *abaya.* A moment later, he was out the door.

"That bastard is as dirty as they come," Paxton said as Bolan sat down and opened up the laptop. He called up the map of Amsterdam, then zoomed in on the area around the Amstel. Another beeping blip appeared on the screen, and both he and Paxton could see that Hassan was just leaving the hotel.

Bolan zoomed in as tight as he could, squinting slightly as his eyes moved from the hotel toward the coffeehouse Hassan had described. Next to it, he could see the old abandoned castle the informant had mentioned. He watched the dot as Hassan began walking that way.

"So far, so good," Paxton said. The two men watched as the informant turned the final corner and came to the coffeehouse. He hesitated for a moment, then went inside. The blinking dot turned solid, which meant the informant had quit moving. He had either found a place to stand or sit.

"I think he's been working against us all along," Paxton said. "Everything he's helped us with has either been a red herring or a trap to get us killed."

"I'm leaning that way myself," Bolan said, "but we could still be wrong. And even if we aren't, he can still be useful to us."

"You want to tell me *how?*" Paxton asked.

"Once we're *sure* he's dirty, I have my own ways of getting information out of men like him," Bolan said quietly.

"I hope I get to help," said the Ranger.

The Executioner didn't answer—just continued to watch the spot on the screen. Every so often it blinked, which only meant that Hassan had changed his sitting position, crossed his leg or moved some other body part. The dot itself wasn't moving.

Kurtzman and Schwarz had done their usual excellent job of coming up with effective, pragmatic, and state-of-the-art technical gear.

But thirty minutes later, the dot did begin to blink as Hassan exited the coffeehouse. Bolan and Paxton watched the dot stop on the sidewalk. Then, instead of starting back *toward* them, the postage stamp homer told them that the informant was going the *other way*.

"What do you think's up?" Paxton asked.

"Your guess is as good as mine," said Bolan.

The dot didn't go far before it stopped again, just outside the walls around the castle that Hassan had mentioned. There was a pause in the blinking, which probably meant he was standing there, looking at the castle walls. When the blinks began again, Bolan and Paxton watched the dot cut down the street between the castle and the coffeehouse, then turn down what the on-screen map identified as an alley at the rear of the castle. It stopped again for a few seconds, then Hassan walked on, completely circling the castle walls until he was back in the alley again.

"What in hell's name is going on?" Paxton asked rhetorically.

The blinking stopped once more, the dot staying in place for a second.

"He's climbing over a gate," Bolan said, pointing to the tiny rectangle on the map that signified the opening. "My guess is the walls are too high and slick to climb."

"Then the son of a bitch *really is* meeting someone," Paxton said. Both men watched the dot on the screen as it started across the open ground between the walls and the castle proper. Then Hassan appeared to enter the castle itself. "He's snitching us off *again*."

"Maybe," said the Executioner. "Maybe not." The knot in his belly told him that while things didn't look good for the informant, this was no time to jump to conclusions.

Bolan stood up. "Whatever he's doing there, we need to find out *now*. And we aren't going to do that by staying here and watching this screen. So grab your trench coat while I get into my blacksuit." The Executioner's vest, sweater and jeans came off and his blacksuit went back on. So did the trench coat and trouser legs that had been cut just above the knees and were held in place beneath the tail of the coat with rubber bands. He grabbed the laptop as Paxton pulled his false trouser legs over his boots and secured them with his own rubber bands, then stuffed the small computer into its padded case and slipped the carry sling over his shoulder. The two men started toward the door.

Suddenly the Executioner stopped. Turning over his shoulder, he said, "Bring the bag with our Arab clothes in it, too, Paxton. No telling what situation we may run into."

The Army Ranger backtracked to the corner and lifted the large black nylon case. A second after that they were out of the door in the hallway.

"It took you long enough to get here," Dawud A. said in Arabic, his voice holding a scolding tone.

"Well, I couldn't just pick up and leave," said the man who followed him down the castle stairs in the same language. "I'm *watched*, you know. Besides that, I think they've grown even more suspicious of me lately."

"My heart bleeds a thousand drops for you," Dawud said, still sarcastic. Then his voice changed. "At least you are here now. I am anxious to identify the real Phillip Paxton and put him to work building the dirty bomb. Did you see the truck that just arrived in back of the castle?"

"I saw it," said the other man, who was disguised in a *kaffiyeh* and *abaya*. "It contains the radioactive material you need?"

"It does, indeed." Dawud smiled as they reached the bottom of the steps and turned left on the cold stone floor. "Now all I will have to do is get this American Phillip Paxton to put the pieces together and form a bomb. We can make Amsterdam uninhabitable for a century or so. Not to mention all of the infidel lives—thousands, if not a hundred thousand or so—lost before the city can be evacuated. Praise Allah."

"Yes," said Dawud's companion. "Allah be praised. Just give me time to get out of town before you light the fuse. I plan to serve Allah *alive* for a good long time."

Dawud turned on the man suddenly, reaching out and grabbing him by the front of his *abaya*. Lifting him almost off his feet, he said, "Do not *ever* let me hear you blaspheme the name of Allah again, or I will forget that you have been of service to us and kill you with my bare hands. You may *say* you are Islamic but you are not. Your belief in Allah and the prophet are only an excuse to sell your services to us and other true believers."

"Hey, slow down!" said the man in the *kaffeyeh*.

Dawud dropped the other man and shoved him against the wall. "You believe only in *yourself* and the money you make," he almost spit. "You have been well paid for what you have done for us, and that is the only reason you have done it." He started off down the cold stony hallway toward the dungeon again and said over his shoulder. "Now, I want you to identify Phillip Paxton and then get out of here. Your very presence in such a place where Allah's sacred work is done is offensive."

When he reached the dungeon, Dawud motioned for the two men holding the AK-47s to unlock the ancient wooden door. Light from the hallway flooded the darkened room, and it took the man disguised in the *kaffiyeh* only seconds to point his finger and say, "There he is. That's Paxton."

"Bring him out," Dawud ordered the guards.

A moment later, Phil Paxton was unshackled and half dragged from the dungeon as the thick wooden door slammed shut again behind him.

"Take him to the examination room," Dawud said. "And stay with him until I arrive." His loud, annoying laugh made the disguised man want to cover his ears. "I suspect I will have to be at least somewhat persuasive with this American before I can convince him to do my bidding."

Dawud and his visitor followed Phil Paxton and the guards down the hallway until they came to the steps leading upward. The guards continued on with their prisoner, but Dawud and the other man in the *abaya* mounted the steps.

At the top of the stairs, Dawud led his companion into a small office near the front of the castle. Opening the top drawer of his desk, he revealed several stacks of American hundred-dollar bills wrapped in thick paper bands. Taking a handful of the stacks out of the drawer, he practically threw them at the other man. "Here," he said. "In addition to what you have already been paid, this is for coming to identify him."

The man tucked the money inside his robe and said, "Thank you."

"You know the way out," Dawud said.

The other man nodded, then disappeared from the room.

Dawud opened another drawer and pulled out a wickedly curved *jambiya*. He tested the edge by shaving off a portion of the thick hair on his left arm, then smiled. Even now, the radioactive material—packed tightly in airtight steel containers—was being unloaded at the rear of the castle. To anyone watching, it would look innocent enough. But as an extra level of security, Dawud had made sure no one could see what was going on. Even though they were in the heart of Amsterdam, the high walls that surrounded the castle blocked all view.

Sheathing the *jambiya*, Dawud dropped it inside his *abaya* and walked around the desk to the stone corridor outside again. Turning down the steps that led back down to the dungeon and examination room, he smiled to himself.

By now, the guards would have Phil Paxton strapped down and ready in the examination room. And even if the

American proved soft and agreed to help build the dirty bomb immediately, Dawud still planned to do at least a *little* cutting with the *jambiya*. No matter how cooperative Paxton proved to be, he wanted the American to at least experience some of the pain the Islamic world lived with on a day-to-day basis, which was caused by his country, the Great Satan America.

Dawud had no doubt that creating that pain was the right thing to do.

After all, it was all in the name of Allah.

STILL CLAD IN BLACKSUITS and trench coats, Bolan and Paxton cut down the alley that lead behind the coffeehouse and castle, squatting behind a large white trash bin. The Executioner had left the laptop on, running on batteries, and now he pulled it from the padded case and opened it to look at the screen.

The tiny homing device was still inside the castle, but it wasn't moving or blinking. Was Hassan meeting with a Hands of Allah representative even now?

"I'm putting a bullet in that bastard's brain the second I see him," Paxton said through clenched teeth as he watched the screen over the Executioner's shoulder. "Look at that. The bastard is talking to someone, giving us up right now."

"You may be right," Bolan said. "On the other hand, I want him alive. At least long enough to question." He paused, then added, "After that, if he's been working both sides of the fence, he's all yours."

"I'm gonna hold you to that promise," Paxton said, his face grim.

Bolan glanced up and down the alley. They were still a good two blocks away from both the coffeehouse and castle, and there was no one in sight. "This is as good a place as any to ditch the trench coats and get into our robes," he said.

"Why?" Paxton asked. "If we're going to bust into the castle, guns blazing, what's it matter if—"

"It matters," said the Executioner as he shrugged out of his trench coat, stood up and dropped it into the trash bin at his side. "I want to stick my head into the coffeehouse for a second before we go onto the castle."

"Why?" Paxton asked. But it was already obvious that he would follow the Executioner's lead because his trench coat was coming off, too.

"Because if the building turns out to be a machine shop or a pet store or a beauty salon, there'll be *no doubt* that Hassan was lying to us."

"And if it really is a coffeehouse?" Paxton asked as he began to put on his *abaya*.

"Then we still won't know for sure," said the Executioner. "It could go either way."

When the two men were appropriately dressed again, they walked side by side on down the alley. When they came to the back door of the coffeehouse, the Executioner could smell the strong aroma of Turkish coffee coming through the screen door. That didn't mean it was actually a coffeehouse, he knew. Ninety percent of all the Arabic stores and other establishments in Amsterdam kept a pot on the go all day long no matter what their business.

Standing to the side of the screen, the Executioner glanced in and saw a large kitchen. Six large coffeepots were lined up on a counter, and several men dressed similarly to him and Paxton were busily served tiny ceramic cups and cooked food.

That was enough to convince both the Executioner and Paxton. It *was* a coffeehouse. At least that part of Hassan's story had proved true. The two men moved down the alley toward the rear of the castle.

"So we don't know any more than we did before," Paxton whispered in a dejected tone.

Bolan didn't answer until they had crossed the street between the castle and the coffeehouse and begun walking along the high rear wall. Roughly twenty yards from the corner, the Executioner could see an opening—the entrance to the grounds that had been on the laptop map. Walking on as if they were just two more Arabs out for a stroll, they saw a pair of men standing just inside the rusty iron gate.

Both men wore appropriate Muslim garb, but they also gripped AK-47s in their hands.

"When we come abreast of the gate," the Executioner said to Paxton, "say something to them in Arabic. Anything to take their minds off what we're doing for a second or so."

The men with the Soviet assault rifles saw them coming and moved to the edge of the gate, their weapons held in the low-ready position. Bolan let the tail of his *kaffiyeh* hang in front of his face and looked down as they approached. Out of the corner of his eye, he could see that Paxton was rubbing his cheek to partially hide his own Euro-American features, as well. They stopped at the gate and Paxton spit out something in Arabic.

As the words came out of his mouth, the Beretta 93-R came out from under the Executioner's *abaya*. He thumbed the selector switch to semiauto rather than 3-round-burst mode and put one lone 9 mm slug into the head of both men.

The two men slumped over the gate, as dead as the iron that held them up.

"Quick," the Executioner said, grabbing one of the men by the shoulders. "Pull them over and get them into the alley, out of sight."

Bolan and Paxton jerked the lifeless bodies over the railing and dropped them to the sides of the gate where they couldn't be seen from the castle. The Executioner looked downward. Both men's robes were similar to their own, but the tails of their headdresses were striped instead of plain. "Swap headdresses with them," Bolan said quickly, and a second later it had been done. Then, picking up the AK-47s, which had fallen at the foot of the gate, the Executioner and Army Ranger climbed over the low bars as it appeared Hassan had done earlier when they'd tracked him on the screen.

That memory wasn't lost on Paxton. "If these guys were here when Abdul showed up," he said, "they let him in."

The implication wasn't lost on Bolan, and again he had to agree that things didn't look good for Hassan. On the other hand, his gut told him not to jump to any conclusions. There were other possibilities of which he and Paxton couldn't possibly be aware.

Across the yard, at the rear of the castle, the Executioner could see a large two-ton truck. It had been backed up to the edge of the castle, and men were unloading steel boxes. The boxes might not have been labeled but Bolan had seen them before. They were the airtight containers used to hold radioactive waste.

Bolan and Paxton kept their faces as covered as possible as they strolled across the yard as if they owned it. The Executioner studied the truck. If this nuclear waste material was being unloaded at the site, it had to mean that this was where Phil Paxton was being held. It also had to mean that the Hands of Allah had somehow learned that Paxton was more than capable of helping them build a dirty bomb.

But how had they gotten such information about Phil Paxton? Another possibility in addition to Abdul's supposed guilt began to form in the Executioner's mind. He pushed it to the back of his brain. Right now it wasn't as important as the here and now.

If the material for a dirty bomb was just now arriving, it probably meant that the terrorists had only recently realized that they'd accidentally stumbled upon such a prize in the younger Paxton. And there had not yet been time to force Phil into constructing any weapons of mass destruction.

It was obvious that Brick Paxton had been thinking along the same lines when he whispered, "This doesn't mean they aren't in there skinning him alive right now to let him know they're serious."

Bolan nodded but didn't answer. "Sling your rifle like you're just on your way to the bathroom or something," he said.

Paxton understood the Executioner's reasoning and did so. Bolan reached back into his *abaya* and kept his hand on the Beretta's grips. They passed the men unloading the truck without getting even one second glance.

Such was not the case when they entered the castle proper, however.

Another traditionally dressed man holding an AK-74 across his body stood guard at the rear door as they approached. He obviously recognized the headdresses Bolan and Paxton had acquired but knew something was wrong.

"Salih?" he said. "Thabit?" By the time the last name was out of his mouth, he had realized that the men approaching him might have on their clothes, but they were not Salah or Thabit. He had also seen their faces, which weren't even Arab, and started to turn his rifle toward them.

Bolan put an end to that with a quick 9 mm slug between the man's eyes. The guard fell to the ground just outside the castle.

Bolan and Paxton stepped over him and entered what had probably been the great room when the castle had been constructed centuries earlier. Banquets, balls, and other parties would have been held in this room.

But now, it had been turned into a weapons-storage area

and the Executioner not only saw stacks of various rifles and handguns but also cases of Semtex plastique and other explosives.

Four more men stood guard in the great room and, once again, Bolan and Paxton did their best to keep their faces hidden as they approached them. Obviously not expecting trouble—did that mean Hassan had *not* exposed them?—three of the men had gathered to converse and laugh near a door leading out of the room. Bolan moved that way while Paxton started toward a fourth man at another doorway twenty yards away.

The laughing, talking men didn't look up until the Executioner was twenty feet away. As they turned toward him, the grins on their faces faded and they grabbed for their slung rifles. They were two slow.

Still firing the sound-suppressed Beretta on semiauto, Bolan put a 9 mm RBCD round into the skulls of all three men. As the last one fell, Bolan looked to Paxton.

The U.S. Army Ranger had thrust the four-inch blade of the cactus-handled dagger into the very center of the fourth guard's chest. Now, he was working it up and down, back and forth, widening the wound. The short-bladed dagger could have only barely entered the heart, but Paxton was making the most of it. And his most appeared to be good enough as he pushed his opponent back against the wall, withdrew the Damascus blade, then brought it across the man's throat for good measure.

Bolan motioned the Ranger over to him and Paxton hurried that way. "We keep this quiet as long as we can," he said, "but sooner or later, someone's going to get a shot off. When that happens, we'll go to the loud guns, too. You ready?"

"I'm ready to get my brother out of here," Paxton said, his jaw set firm.

Bolan nodded, then stepped out from the great room into a hallway. Ten yards away, he saw a set of stone steps leading down into the bowels of the castle. The place undoubtedly had been built with a dungeon. And that would still be the most likely place to hold prisoners. Leading the way, he heard Paxton's boots walking softly behind him.

They couldn't hold the tails of their *kaffiyehs* over their faces and keep the AK-47s ready at the same time, especially with Bolan still holding the sound-suppressed Beretta in one hand and his rifle in the other. So he and Paxton let the cloth fall from their faces.

As they walked along the underground corridor, they saw a man dressed much as they were come out of a doorway a good thirty yards away. He stood sideways to them, which meant the tails of *his* headdress *did* block out most of his features. When he saw them, he stopped in his tracks. Pulling a small mini-Glock pistol from under his robe, the man started to bring it up into play.

Bolan ended the attempt with another quiet burp from the Beretta. They continued on toward the steps leading downward. The man with the Glock had fallen a good twenty yards on past them, and he wasn't moving.

Suddenly, another man wearing full Arab dress seemed to step out of nowhere and fire a full-auto burst of 7.62 mm rounds from his AK-47. The man was frightened and fired wildly, with none of the bullets striking either Bolan or Paxton.

But he did accomplish one thing before the Executioner took him down with another sound-suppressed round from the Beretta.

Now everyone in the castle and outside in the yard knew intruders had invaded.

TWO MORE MEN DRESSED in traditional Arabic garb emerged through doorways somewhere down the hall. Even in their own Arab disguises, Bolan and Paxton were recognized as outsiders immediately. The two terrorists fired at the same time, and a hailstorm of bullets came at the two Americans, buzzing like angry wasps, striking the stone walls and sending sparks throughout the hallway.

Both Bolan and Paxton dropped to their knees to make smaller targets, then returned fire with the AK-47s they'd taken from the guards at the gate.

Bolan's first burst struck a Hands of Allah gunner squarely in the chest, turning his white *abaya* a dark red with blood straight from the heart. As he raised his rifle, taking aim at the second man, the Executioner saw his target already in a macabre dance of death from Paxton's rifle.

The Executioner didn't waste any more rounds. Although both he and Paxton had refilled their 50- and 100-round Calico magazines back at the Hotel Amstel, and had plenty of ammo on hand in addition to their sidearms, the longer-barreled AK-47s were easier to point at the longer range within the castle's corridors, and Bolan wanted to conserve as many of the Russian rounds as possible.

Heading toward the stone staircase, Bolan and Paxton encountered no more Hands of Allah followers. But as the Executioner turned to sprint down the steps, another round whistled past the side of his face. He looked down the steps, to the floor below, and saw a terrorist aiming a Makarov pistol his way, riding the recoil of the first shot and preparing to take a second.

Like his friend had been earlier, he was too slow. But, then, so were most men compared to the Executioner.

Bolan put a single round between the man's eyes. The force threw the man backward, and the Executioner continued down the steps with Paxton at his heels. As he neared the underground portion of the castle, he heard gunfire behind him. Turning, he saw that yet another Hands of Allah terror-

ist had emerged out of hiding and slipped quietly to the steps.
Paxton had caught him squarely in the chest, and he tumbled
forward down the staircase.

The Executioner approached the lower level cautiously. More
of the enemy were down here; there had to be. His instincts told
him that there was no longer any doubt that Phil Paxton and the
other American hostages were being held somewhere nearby.
As to whether Abdul Hassan had set them up, he still had no idea.

Finally stepping down off the last stone stair, Bolan saw
that the hallway led both right and left. The Executioner
speculated that the dungeon itself would be to the left. Following his instincts, he came to a bend in the hallway and
stopped, peering around the corner.

Two men stood in front of a thick and ancient wooden door
that had a small window at eye level with tiny iron bars set
into it. The guards at the door had to have heard the gunfire
from above, and would have heard more as it headed their
way. One held AK-47 aimed directly down the hall. The other
had an American-made M-16.

Bolan waved behind him, motioning for Paxton to stop and
cover their rear. A quick glance over his shoulder told him the
Ranger had already done so, facing away from the Executioner with his AK-47 stock against his shoulder and the barrel
pointing down the hall.

The guards in front of the door were expecting them, and
there would be no element of surprise. On the other hand, the
Executioner had more than one trick up his sleeve, and he used
one of them now. Holding the AK-47 high over his head, he
stayed behind the bend in the underground tunnel but stuck
the rifle out, pointed toward the dungeon door. Cutting loose
with a steady stream of autofire, he heard return fire come
back at him and saw the rounds set off more sparks as they
struck the stone wall on past him.

Immediately dropping to one knee, the Executioner leaned around the corner this time and took aim. It looked as if one of his earlier, "high and blind" rounds had already taken one of the Hands of Allah guards in the knee, and the man bent over painfully. Holding the trigger back on the AK, the Executioner sprayed a figure eight back and forth between the two men until both were dead on the floor.

Bolan rose back to his feet. "Follow me, but keep covering our rear," he yelled to Paxton. He turned the corner and sprinted down the corridor to where the dead men were bleeding out. Stepping up to the window, he looked inside and saw several men in chains on the floor. He tried the door. Locked.

The Executioner dropped to one knee again, this time searching through the robes of the two guards he'd just shot. He finally found a huge ring with several large, ancient keys on it, threaded through the guard's belt beneath his robe. Jerking the Ka-bar knife from behind his back, he severed the belt and took the key ring.

The second key he tried opened the ancient lock and the door. Bolan stepped inside. "Anybody want to go home?" he asked.

The question was met with a round of cheers.

"Which one of you is Phil Paxton?" the Executioner asked.

"They took him out about a half hour ago," one of the men, shackled in the corner, said in a weary voice. "They'd been trying to figure out which one of us was him ever since we got here."

"How'd they finally find him?"

"A guy who must have known him came in and ID'd him," another man said.

"What did this guy look like?" Bolan asked.

"Like all the rest of these bastards," a third man said bitterly. "Long robe and one of those floppy hats with tails."

Bolan had moved into the cell as the conversation took

place and found that one of the other keys fit the padlocks on the belly chains around the men. He hadn't noticed it until now, but there was also a modern handcuff key on the ring that freed the hostages from their cuffs.

As he unlocked the men, the Executioner heard new firing in the hallway. Evidently more Hands of Allah terrorists had turned the corner of the corridor. "You okay, Paxton?" he called out as he freed the last of the chained men.

"Never been better," the Army Ranger shouted back. "But I'll be even better than this if we find my brother."

"We *will* find your brother," the Executioner said.

The men he had just freed began to stand up, but their movements were stiff and slow moving after being chained in place for so long. Some were still exhibiting the signs of being drugged, and Bolan knew he couldn't take them with him as he and Paxton searched the rest of the castle for Phil. The Executioner retrieved the AK-47 and M-16 from the dead guards in the corridor, then stepped back into the dungeon area. "Any of you know how to use these things?" he asked.

"I do," one man said. "I'm in the National Guard."

Bolan handed him the M-16. "Check the bodies outside the door for extra magazines," he said. "Anybody else know how to shoot?" The rest of the men shook their heads. The Executioner handed the AK-47 to the man who appeared most sober and said, "He'll show you how it works." He indicated the National Guardsman. "All of you, stay here until we come back for you."

"But we want out of here *now!*" one of the men almost screamed.

"It's not practical to take you with us yet," Bolan said in the kindest tone of voice he could muster. "But we'll be back for you." Before the man could speak again, he turned and hurried out of the dungeon. Ahead, he saw another cross hall. When he reached the corner, he slowly peered around the side.

Three more Hands of Allah guards were standing outside a doorway. Stepping back away from the corner, the Executioner ejected the magazine from his rifle and inspected it. Only two rounds remained, and he quietly placed it on the floor, pulling the Calico, while holding the 50-round drum mag, out of his *abaya* to the end of the sling.

Without further ado, the Executioner stepped around the corner and pulled the trigger as far back as he could. The quick-firing automatic machine pistol sprayed the hallway ahead like some wind from hell. Moving the muzzle back and forth, the Executioner knew he had fired at least half of his 50-round drum by the time the third guard had fallen on the floor.

Keeping his back against the wall, the Calico still pointed ahead of him and ready, Bolan moved cautiously toward the trio of dead men. As he neared, he saw the open door into one of the rooms.

And a lone man stood between two long steel tables such as might be found in a doctor's office or surgery room. The man was staring at the doorway, but his only visible weapon was a wickedly curved *jambiya* knife.

Two men were strapped down on the tables, fully prepared for whatever tortures the man with the *jambiya* was planning to inflict upon them.

The Executioner stepped into the doorway, the Calico ready in case the man between the tables had some hidden firearm. The man's positioning hid the face of the hostage on the table behind him, but strapped to the steel closest to Bolan, the Executioner could see an American who resembled Brick Paxton. Not as many battle scars on his face and arms, perhaps, but definitely the man's brother.

It didn't appear that Phil Paxton had been harmed yet, but there was no doubt that had Bolan and Paxton not arrived when they did, he was going to be.

"Come here," the Executioner told Brick Paxton over his shoulder.

The Army Ranger complied. And when he did, and saw his brother, strapped down on the shining steel table, a wide grin spread across his face. "Hey, Phil," he said.

"Howdy, big brother," said the man on the table. "What took you so long?"

A sudden snarl came from the man holding the *jambiya*. He brought it high over his head, ready to plunge it into Phil Paxton's chest. "Shoot me if you must," he said in a contemptuous voice. "But unless your aim is perfect, I will still send this man to Hell before I go immediately to Paradise where fifty virgins await my every beck and call."

Bolan lifted the Calico slightly, lining the sights up so that his first shot would strike the Hands of Allah man in the brain stem, shutting down all motor skills and activity immediately. In the corner of his eye, he saw that Paxton had seen his movement and knew that Phil was in no immediate danger. Not anymore.

"I will still kill this man who says he is your brother," warned the man with the *jambiya*. He had no idea how accurately the Executioner could shoot.

"I've got a better idea," said Brick Paxton, shoving the Calico back under his *abaya* and drawing the cactus-handled, Damascus-steel dagger his brother had given him for his birthday. "You've got a knife, I've got a knife. How about we play a little one-on-one? If you kill me, my partner will let you go." He turned to Bolan for confirmation.

The Executioner nodded. Brick Paxton had earned the right to do whatever he wanted with the man between the two tables in front of them.

"What's your name?" Paxton demanded as he stepped forward, dagger in hand.

"Dawud A.," said the man with the *jambiya,* stepping out from between the tables.

Brick Paxton took a knife-fighting stance, his dagger held low, the tip pointed directly up at Dawud's eyes. "So you're the famous Dawud A." He laughed out loud. "Tell me, how'd your community service go after that assassination attempt you were convicted of? Hope it was good. Because this time, you're getting a lethal injection. The only difference is the injection will be steel from a much larger needle than they usually use."

The two men began to circle each other. Brick Paxton held the dagger saber-style while Dawud clutched his *jambiya* downward in a reverse grip. Paxton was smiling the whole time, and Bolan could see that the man had been well-trained in what was becoming an almost archaic art—knife-on-knife fighting.

The fight didn't take long.

Like a well-honed boxing counterpuncher, Brick Paxton let Dawud A. make the first move. The Hand of Allah leader brought the *jambiya* around in an arc, aiming the edge of his weapon at Paxton's midsection. Paxton leaned back slightly, hollowed out his stomach and hunched his back. He used what knife fighters call the "live" hand—his empty one—to guide the *jambiya* harmlessly on past him. But as he did, the hand holding the cactus-handled dagger shot forward, slicing through Dawud's wrist and causing the terrorist to drop his weapon.

The Army Ranger didn't wait for his opponent to pick his knife up again. Stepping in, he drove the needle point of the Damascus blade into the middle of Dawud's throat. Then, with the steel still inside the man's flesh, he ripped the knife to the side, severing arteries, ligaments, and everything else the razor-edged blade encountered.

A fire-hose spray of blood blew out of Dawud's neck as the man tumbled to the floor. He thrashed about on the floor for a few seconds. Then he lay still.

Brick Paxton stepped forward, using his bloodstained dagger to sever the leather restraints that held his brother to the table.

Phil looked at the bloody blade. "Damn," he said. "I'm glad I bought you the knife for your birthday instead of the tie and socks I'd been looking at." As soon as the leather had been cut, he sat up, and the two brothers embraced.

And the Executioner saw a sight rarely seen by any man. A battle-hardened U.S. Army Ranger crying his eyes out like a baby.

But there was more to be done. When Dawud had moved out from between the tables for the knife fight, Bolan had seen the face of the man tied to the other table. Abdul Hassan. Walking quickly toward him, Bolan drew his Ka-bar fighting knife and severed the straps holding Hassan in place. The informant sat up and started to speak.

Bolan held up a hand. "You can tell us all about it when we get out of here," he said, "which we need to do *now*, before the cops come. The people around the castle would have to be deaf not to have heard all of this gunfire."

Turning, the Executioner led the way, the Calico ahead of him just in case they had missed any of the terrorists on their way down. When he reached the top of the steps, he looked through a window and saw that while the steel boxes of radioactive nuclear waste were still stacked in the yard behind the castle, the truck and the men who had unloaded it were long gone.

Sometimes a few of them got away. And sooner or later, Bolan would encounter those men again. When he did, they'd meet the same fate as the Hands of Allah terrorists strewed all over the old castle.

Bolan hurried down the hall to examine the man who had emerged while he was still using the sound-suppressed Beretta. It was the man who had stood sideways to them, the tail of his *kaffiyeh* hiding his face as he drew the mini-Glock from under his robe.

The Executioner wasn't surprised at what he found when he moved the tails of the headdress to the side. There, lying wide-eyed in death, was a face with which he was all too familiar. The face of a traitor whose actions had made him and Paxton suspect, and Paxton almost kill, Abdul Hassan.

Below him, dead on the cold stone floor, lay CIA operative Felix Young.

Epilogue

Bolan held the cell phone to his ear. "Okay, Barb," he said. "Have Hal call me as soon as he gets back, okay?"

"Okay, Striker. Will do."

The Executioner folded the phone shut and took a seat in the armchair he'd dozed in earlier in the day. Seated around the coffee table, drinking coffee they had brewing in the kitchenette, were the rest of the men. Abdul Hassan sat in the recliner, with Brick and Phil Paxton on the couch to the side.

"So, Abdul," the Executioner said as he took his seat. "Answer a few questions for me now that it's over."

"I will be happy to do so," Hassan said.

"First, what were you really doing on the cell phone, and then trying to sneak out when you thought we were asleep earlier?" the Executioner asked.

Hassan looked down at the carpet, his face coloring slightly. "I had an idea," he said. "An idea that I came upon suddenly, and that would stop the male relatives of the women I had impregnated from killing me. But I was embarrassed to talk about it in front of men such as yourselves." He had been looking at Bolan and now nodded toward Brick Paxton. "I do not mean this in a condescending way, but you are from another culture and cannot possibly understand mine."

"Don't worry about us understanding," Brick Paxton said. "Just tell us."

"I am going to gather up the women I have impregnated, then move to Saudi Arabia and marry them all." Hassan smiled.

"How many wives are you going to have?" asked Phil Paxton, who had not been around when Hassan's personal life began interfering with the mission.

"Well," Hassan said. "I know of three who are with child."

"You're going to have quite a harem," said the Executioner. "Now, tell me why you went into the castle on your own instead of coming back to the room to get us."

"I was lucky in the coffeehouse," Hassan said. "I learned almost immediately that many men in traditional dress were often seen coming and going from the castle. I knew you were disappointed in the work I had done for you so far, and I had sensed that you were even suspecting me of being in league with the Hands of Allah. I wanted something *concrete* to bring back to you. So I walked around the castle walls. The second time I came to the gate, I was suddenly jerked over it by two men who were acting as guards. It seemed they were suspicious of me and planned to take no chances."

"So you wound up on one of the torture tables like me," Phil Paxton said. "I wonder who Dawud A. was planning on cutting up first, me or you?"

"I do not know," said Hassan. "And I will be happy to live the rest of my life without that information."

"Back at the log cabin," Bolan said. "When we looked through the windows we could still hear you arguing, but some of the men were smiling. That didn't make sense."

"It was exactly like I told you," Hassan answered. "They found the recorder and transmitter almost immediately. They knew there must be some kind of surveillance team nearby, and wanted to lure you in. Some of them, even though they were shouting angrily, were smiling because they thought they were so clever."

"They didn't look all that clever when we left," Brick Paxton said.

"Dead men rarely do," Hassan agreed.

Bolan stood up, walked to the kitchenette and poured himself another cup of coffee. "Anybody else want more?" he asked.

The rest of the men in the room shook their heads.

When he'd returned to his chair, Bolan said, "In hindsight, it's easy to see what happened. Felix Young was nearing retirement and didn't plan to live on what the government was going to send him every month. So he sold out. He'd have had access to U.S. government files the average person didn't, and my guess is he began running checks on all Americans flying into Amsterdam. When he found out what Phil did for a living, he knew he'd struck gold."

"But why did they kidnap the other men?" Phil asked.

"Cover," his brother said. "To make it look like you were just another random snatch." He paused and took a sip of his coffee. "That, and the fact that bastards like that just plain like what they do."

Phil looked across the table at Hassan. "Congratulations on your…marriages, I guess you'd say," he said. "I'm going home and getting married myself."

"Ah, then congratulations are in order for you, too," said Abdul Hassan.

"Well," Bolan said. "Except for dozing in this chair while I kept an eye open to see what Abdul might be up to, I haven't slept in about three days." He stood up, set his coffee cup back down on the table and started toward one of the bedrooms. He was halfway there when his cell phone rang.

"Yeah," the Executioner said into the phone.

"Good job, big guy," Hal Brognola said. "Barb just filled

me in on the details. I made a couple of calls, and the CIA is sending someone to pick up those nuclear waste containers right now."

"Good," Bolan said. "I'm gonna grab a little slee—"

Brognola interrupted him. "By the way," he said. "You need to get your butt to the airport as fast as possible. Jack Grimaldi should be landing there in a few minutes to pick you up. There's a situation developing in Russia right now."

Bolan couldn't help but chuckle. "Okay, Hal," he said. "I'll pack and head out." He folded the phone shut again.

"You got to leave?" Brick Paxton said.

Bolan nodded as he changed directions and headed toward the luggage and equipment bags in the corner. He needed sleep, and needed it badly.

But it would have to come on the plane, as usual, as the Executioner headed into yet another mission.

JAMES AXLER
DEATH LANDS®

Sky Raider

Raw determination in a land of horror...and hope

In the tortured but not destroyed lands of apocalyptic madness of Deathlands, few among the most tyrannical barons can rival the ruthlessness of Sandra Tregart. With her restored biplane, she delivers death from the skies to all who defy her supremacy—a virulent ambition that challenges Ryan Cawdor and his band in unfathomable new ways.

Available June 2007 wherever books are sold.

GOLD EAGLE®

GDL78

∴ James Axler
Outlanders®

SKULL THRONE

RADIANT EVIL

Buried deep in the Mayan jungle amidst a civilization of lost survivors and emissaries of the dead, lies a relic that hides secrets to the prize—planet Earth. In sinister hands, it guarantees complete and absolute power. Kane and the rebels have just one chance to stop a rogue overlord from seizing glory, but must face an old enemy to stop him.

Available May 2007, wherever you buy books.

TAKE 'EM FREE
2 action-packed novels plus a mystery bonus
NO RISK
NO OBLIGATION TO BUY

JAKE STRAIT

THE DEVIL KNOCKS

BY FRANK RICH

HELL IS FOR THE LIVING

It is 2031, the hellscape of the future where chemical and biological cesspools have created everybody's worst nightmare. In the corner of hell known as Denver, Jake Strait must face a bounty hunter turned revolutionary in a flat-out race for the finish line, where even victory will place him in double jeopardy.

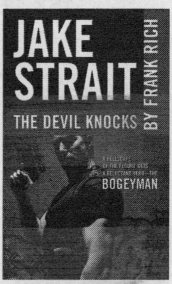

Available April 2007, wherever you buy books.

AleX Archer
THE LOST SCROLLS

In the right hands, ancient knowledge can save a struggling planet...

Ancient scrolls recovered among the charred ruins of the Library of Alexandria reveal astonishing knowledge that could shatter the blueprint of world energy—and archaeologist Annja Creed finds herself an unwilling conspirator in a bid for the control of power.

Available May 2007 wherever you buy books.

GOLD EAGLE